detective
DOT

Written by
{Sophie_Deen}
and her friends

Chapter 1:

{Detective_Dot}

Clink.

Clank.

CLUNK!

"There," said Dot, giving her selfie stick one last twist of the screwdriver. "That's the MegaFart installed."

"Impressive!" beeped her flying sidekick, Drone, as she scanned the gadget with her sensors.

It was a selfie stick, but not just any old selfie stick. Dot had built it herself, and packed it with surprises. "If anyone but me tries using it, the MegaFart is unleashed*," Dot explained, pointing to the thumbprint sensor. "This might be my best invention yet!"

Drone's speakers crackled with static.

"Except you, obviously," Dot added quickly. Making a farting selfie stick had been easy compared to building Drone. It had taken all Dot's skill to pack so many gadgets into Drone's little titanium body while keeping her light enough to fly with just one propellor. "Let's test the remote control!"

Dot ran her finger down a touch sensor. The selfie stick handle opened, revealing hidden gizmos inside. She pressed a button and the TV across the room sprang into life.

"Very impressive!" chirped Drone. "You'd better upload the design to the CIAhub."

"You know it!" cried Dot excitedly.

The CIAhub was the central **database** of the CIA – the Children's Intelligence Agency. Run by a shadowy group of child geniuses, with headquarters in an unknown location, the CIA investigated global mysteries, injustices and rotten teachers. No one ever suspected kids, which

*See page 117
for the Selfie_Stick_Code

explained how the CIA had managed to bring down some of the most sophisticated criminal networks in the world. The work was difficult and sometimes dangerous – a recent investigation into rising ice cream prices had ended with an agent being wedgied to within an inch of his life.

Dot had been in the CIA for three years. Her tech skills and stealthiness had helped her become one of their top agents. Even more useful though, was her secret ability...

...Dot could talk to technology.

It had been that way for as long as she could remember. If it used **code**, she could probably speak to it. Code was the language that computers spoke in, so maybe Dot had this gift because she was fluent in code too, or maybe it was a magical power?

Dot glanced over her shoulder – her dad and sister knew nothing about the CIA, and she certainly didn't want them catching her talking to a selfie stick. "Can you hear me?" she whispered.

Then she listened very carefully, because this was the important part – anyone can speak to an object, but only Dot listened for answers. She listened and listened, but the selfie stick said nothing. Dot didn't know why, but some technology talked back and some didn't. Was the selfie stick shy? Did it speak a different language? Were Dot's ears too waxy?

"Oh well," Dot shrugged. "It'll still be perfect for my next CIA mission."

"I hope it's a safe mission for once," muttered Drone.

The TV's volume suddenly shot up and a familiar logo exploded onto the screen. Dot groaned.

Chapter 2:

{Shelly_Belly_on_Telly}

"Shelly Belly!" squeaked Drone, excitedly bouncing in the air. "I love her!"

"*Four-elevenths off! Buy six, get two-and-a-half free! Eighteen for the price of £12.75!*" came a voice from the TV.

A teenage girl with a scarily wide smile burst onto the screen riding a hoverboard. She was dressed in smart black sandals, smart black trousers, and a smart white top. Her hair was bleached white – the latest fashion (apparently) – and she carried an albino micro-pig under her arm. The only bit of colour was her piercing blue eyes.

"Heyyyyya guys, it's me! Your favourite superstar, Shelly Belly! But you knew that already." Shelly winked at the camera. Drone's screen winked back. *"I'm here to give you the lowdown on the hottest new products from the biggest and best shop in the world – Shelly Inc.!"* Shelly squealed, in a horrible, sing-song voice.

Dot hammered the selfie stick's TV remote, but the TV wouldn't turn off. Drat! Inventions always took a while to get right.

"Check out this summer's biggest must-have..."

Shelly pulled a long silver pole out from behind her back.

"...The Selfie Stick Plus! Now even longer!"

Dot pulled a Level 4 Scowl. It looked just like her new invention! Shelly snapped herself from every angle with it, while blabbing on about its features. It had a bendy pole to get your best angle, a special mirror for bum-checking, auto-filters, and even a built-in nose-hair trimmer.

"Nowhere near as good as mine," Dot snorted.

"I don't know," said Drone. "Shelly Belly's a very smart inventor."

"Name me one good creation of hers," Dot retorted

– then immediately regretted it. Drone had Shelly's Clickireadia page saved to her hard drive. Drone waffled on about how Shelly had started out as an inventor, selling her creations online at ShellyInc.com. Thanks to products like Hairy Dairy (furry milk bottles) and TV-Shirts (T-shirts with TVs built in), her site had quickly become the most popular online shop in the world.

Shelly had become the youngest-ever boss of a global business, even before her most famous invention: LavNav, an app for finding the nearest toilet. It had been so popular that Shelly had shot straight from millionaire to trillionaire without even stopping at billionaire.

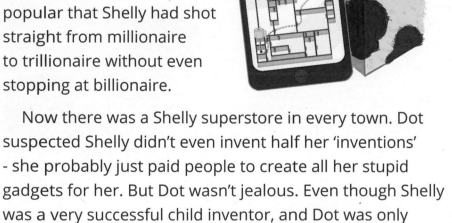

Now there was a Shelly superstore in every town. Dot suspected Shelly didn't even invent half her 'inventions' - she probably just paid people to create all her stupid gadgets for her. But Dot wasn't jealous. Even though Shelly was a very successful child inventor, and Dot was only a quite successful one, Dot definitely, definitely wasn't jealous.

But Dot would love it if the CIA asked her to investigate Shelly. There must be something underhand about how she got everyone to buy her rubbish. Maybe she was secretly brainwashing people? Shelly even sponsored school lessons now!

"Surprise!" cried Shelly's grinning face, louder than ever. *"Deal of the week! Buy four computers, get a fifth free. Because we love you!"*

"Who'd be silly enough to fall for that?" scoffed Dot. She made a final tweak to the remote control in the selfie stick and at last the TV turned off, just as her dad staggered in, his arms piled high with boxes.

"Good news, Odoti!" he boomed. Dad always used her full name. "I've bought five computers!"

Dot rolled her eyes as he wiggled through the mountains of other useless Shelly Inc. junk he'd bought.

"There you are!" cried Dot's sister, Anushka, popping up out of nowhere. "Can we go now?"

Dad shrieked in surprise. The computers flew out of his hands and smashed to pieces on the floor. He was left in a pile of broken parts, surrounded by more mice than a block of cheese.

"Wish I'd bought more in case this happened," he said glumly.

"Where are you going, Nush?" Dot asked her sister, spotting her rucksack.

"I'm, er, going to cousin Sirisha's for a study weekend," Anushka stated, shiftily. "These are all my books…"

Dot pulled a suspicious face. Anushka was almost definitely going somewhere fun with her friends, and was just lying to their dad so that he'd let her go.

"We can have a fun weekend together, Odoti!" declared her dad. Groan. His idea of a fun weekend was watching endless Indian films. Dot's dad had grown up in India, so he was fluent in Punjabi, but Dot couldn't speak the language well enough to understand the movies, let alone enjoy them.

"I have to do my homework," Dot lied, trudging upstairs to her room with Drone hovering faithfully after her.

"C'mon Dad, I need a lift," whined Anushka, dragging him out of the door. "Don't touch my stuff!" she shouted after Dot.

Chapter 3:

{Let_Rip}

Dot stepped carefully over the cables and wires, nuts and bolts, books, video games and socks that covered her floor.

"Are we going to do some cleaning?" chirped Drone.

"Of course not!" snorted Dot. "I do need to polish you, though." She scooped up an old blue cloth from the landing and brandished it at Drone.

"No! It's not microfibre! I'll smudge!" Drone tried to dodge, but Dot was too quick for her. She started wiping Drone, but the little robot wiggled from side to side in mid-air.

"Hold still!" said Dot.

Too late.

A stray thread snagged around Drone's propellor. The cloth started unravelling before their eyes. Dot pulled it one way, Drone pulled the other.

Riiiiip!

The cloth tore.

Bump-oof!

Dot fell backwards, landing on her bottom.

Clang-argh!

Drone shot through the air, clattering into the wall.

"Owww!" grumbled Drone. "Did you have to give me touch sensors?"

Picking herself up, Dot finally freed the cloth from Drone. It was ruined now – just a knotted blue ball of string-thin cotton.

"Oh well, it was just some filthy old rag," shrugged Dot.

Instantly, a mouth formed in the centre of the tangle. Strands sewed themselves into an angry scowl and with one huge jump, the cotton ball leapt out of Dot's hands.

"I am no such thing!" bellowed the ball of string, stamping about on two twisted threads, angrily waving another two plaits as if they were arms. "A human finally learns to talk and the first thing she does is call me a rag! I am Tumble, the greatest garment in the world!"

"You can talk?!" asked Dot. "But you're not tech!"

"I most certainly am," he snapped, pointing to his chest. A tiny computer chip with a little screen was hanging on to him by a thread. "Name tapes are so last year. A designer

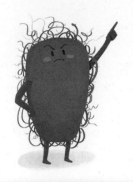

smar-T-shirt like me naturally has a state-of-the-art name chip."

Dot and Drone stared, gawped, gaped. *Designer*? He had to be joking.

"Ah, you're star-struck," he chuckled. Apparently he wasn't joking. "Searching for the courage to ask for an autograph? I'll save you the bother." Snatching up a marker pen from Dot's messy floor, Tumble leapt into the air, landing on top of Drone. "Who shall I make it out to? Tin-head? Crack-pot? Bolt-brains?"

Drone rolled from side to side, beeping frantically as she tried to shake him off. Dot plucked Tumble off her friend before anything else broke.

"Hey Tumble, I'm Detective Dot. Pleased to meet you," said Dot. She placed him safely on the ground and showed him her CIA e-badge – a special ID she'd downloaded onto her phone. "And this is Drone, my..."

Tumble cut her off. "I'm one-of-a-kind, handcrafted by the finest seamstress in the world, Ellyn Shic," he boasted. That sounded oddly familiar – where had Dot heard it before?

Tumble kept blabbering. "I'm made of the purest silk."

Drone zoomed her camera in on his threads. "You're just cheap cotton," she scoffed.

"Nonsense, I'm the height of fashion. But I wouldn't expect something so outdated to understand."

"I'll have you know I'm updated daily with the latest tech," snapped Drone. "You're no designer T-shirt; you're a twisted pile of yarn. And you don't have **Internet access**." She gave one of his stray strands a sharp tug. Tumble yelped when he saw his loose ends.

"What's happened to me?!" he screamed. "I need a mirror! Aha..." He snatched up the selfie stick.

"No!" shouted Dot. Too late.

Click! went the thumbprint sensor button.

BUZZZZ went the selfie-defence mechanism.

PAAAAAARRRRRRRRP! went the MegaFart.

It was a belly-turning smell, ghastlier than a skunk and a dung beetle's breath put together. It was almost as bad as the toilet after Dot's dad had been in.

Gasping for air, Dot threw the window open. Drone used her propellor to blow the foul stench out.

"What on earth was that?" Tumble spluttered.

Dot explained to Tumble all about the selfie stick's thumbprint sensor and MegaFart.

"But I want to snap myself!" Tumble whined.

Dot looked at the grouchy little ball of cotton. It was her fault that he was all unravelled, so perhaps allowing him a few selfies was only fair. She sat down at her desk and unscrewed the selfie stick handle to reveal its inner circuits.

"I just need to rewrite the code so that you can use it," she explained to Tumble.

"Code is the language that computers speak. Unlike me, they can't think for themselves," bragged Drone, jumping at the chance to sound clever. "They just follow specific sets of instructions, called **algorithms**."

"I'd use your thumbprint, but you don't have thumbs..." pondered Dot. She scanned and registered his threads instead. Then she coded new instructions so that the selfie stick would recognise the threads and unlock for him, just as it would for her, without unleashing the MegaFart. What she didn't mention was that he'd only be able to use the camera, because she wasn't giving someone she'd only just met access to all her precious gadgets.

While Dot rewrote the code, Drone made Tumble sign the official CIA Code of Conduct. She made it clear that the selfie stick's camera was meant for crime scene photography, not just endless selfies.

"I wouldn't dream of it," said Tumble as he took a picture of himself. And another. And another... Eventually, three dozen photos later, he spun the camera round to see how he looked. His face fell.

"You've... destroyed me!" he wailed, tugging string down over his face. "Goodbye, photoshoots. Farewell, catwalks. So long, glitz and glamour. My poor owner will never get to wear me again."

"Who actually is your owner?" asked Dot. She pressed a button on his namechip. A word lit up on the screen. A word that made Dot's heart stop and Drone's display flash a huge red warning sign.

"I'm in so much trouble," whimpered Dot.

"You're in so much trouble," whined Drone.

"You were already in trouble," snapped Tumble. "You ruined me, remember!"

"Yes," said Dot. "But I didn't know you were Anushka's!"

Chapter 4:

{Darn_It!}

Dot wasn't scared of her headteacher, or the older kids at school, or even of dentists (they had so many cool gadgets!). But this was different. She'd shredded Anushka's designer smar-T-shirt. Anushka would be back on Sunday and she would be mad.

"Maybe I can fix you!" said Dot desperately. She could put computers back together, so how hard could a T-shirt be?

She grabbed a needle and thread. Tumble shrieked as the light glinted off the sharp point.

"Were you not listening? I was hand-sewn by Ellyn Shic, the finest seamstress in the world. You're not trained! I can't just be put back together like a jigsaw!"

Dot wasn't listening. She was too busy with the needle, stitching and sewing as fast as she could. But Tumble was right.

Despite Dot's best efforts, Tumble only ended up more twisted, tangled and annoyed than ever – and he made sure everyone knew.

"Shrink me! Wear me as pants! Cut my sleeves off and turn me into a vest! Anything but this!" he wailed.

"Can't we sew his mouth shut?" Drone muttered.

Dot's brain was going a mile a minute. There must be some way to mend Tumble before Anushka came home.

"When Dad's watch broke," she said, thinking aloud, "he took it back to the jewellers and they fixed it. If we take Tumble back to where he came from, maybe they can fix him. Where was it, Tumble?"

"I told you," he sighed. "The finest seamstress..."

"In the world. We've got that," interrupted Dot. "We need a bit more detail."

"I might remember more if you hadn't shredded my memories," cried Tumble dramatically.

"There's only one thing for it," declared Dot. "We'll have to investigate!"

Chapter 5:

{Planet_Anushka}

"Anushka told us not to touch her stuff," whined Drone nervously as they sneaked into Dot's sister's room. "We're in enough trouble already."

"So a little more won't hurt," said Dot, not stepping into her sister's room. "Ugh, this place gives me the creeps."

Anushka's room was not like Dot's. There were no half-finished gadgets, tools or blueprints. Anushka didn't stream or download music – she only bought vinyl. Dot couldn't understand why; it was so old it made CDs look modern! Her room was full of weird records by bands no one had heard of.

"I hate vintage," said Tumble, shuddering at a dusty gramophone. "What are we doing here?"

"**Hacking** Nush's email," said Dot casually, firing up her sister's laptop. Anushka bought everything online – it was the only place still selling her strange records. Dot was sure there'd be an email about where she'd bought Tumble. She knew she shouldn't be on Anushka's laptop, but this was an emergency.

The laptop loaded one percent at a time. Nush didn't need a high-spec computer like Dot, because she only used it for downloading black-and-white movies, uploading selfies, writing essays the night before they were due, and generally hogging Dot's bandwidth.

When it finally loaded there was a problem. It was password protected. Dot pondered, and tested a few out.

Imastupidface. Nope. *Badbreath7*. Not that either. *d0tisc00ler*. No.

Cracking this password was harder than Dot had thought.

"Why not just ask it, Little Miss Speaks-to-Tech?" suggested Tumble.

"I ain't saying nothing," growled Anushka's laptop, Sasser.

"We don't really get on," Dot explained quietly. "Not after Drone said baked bean tins had a higher spec..."

"Is there anyone you two don't insult or damage?" asked Tumble.

"Let's try this!" Dot tapped another guess into the keyboard.

"Incorrect!" roared Sasser, enjoying their failure.

 Dot thought hard, staring at Sasser's keyboard. Some letters were sparkly clean but others were so worn away Dot could barely see what letter they were. The U key was almost gone, and so were the S, H and N keys...

Anushka didn't know much about computers, so her password was probably pretty simple. Those letters spelt...

"Nush," Dot typed.

"Er... miles off," said Sasser, but he sounded anxious.

"Maybe if I put a 1 after it?" mused Dot.

"No, no, don't do that," stammered Sasser. His space bar rattled nervously.

"Why not?" asked Dot, suspiciously.

"'Cos it's wrong. Don't waste your time."

"You want us to waste our time," said Dot. She had him there.

Nush1.

Ping!

They were in. Anushka's desktop loaded. Her background was a selfie taken at a gig (she'd told Dad it was a revision night). She was wearing – gulp – a bright blue T-shirt.

"There I am!" cried Tumble. "I'm her favourite, kept for special occasions."

Before he started complaining again, Dot loaded Anushka's email. Thankfully, her silly sister had used the same password. A quick search for 'smar-T-shirt', and Dot found the email she was after. Anushka had bought Tumble from – where else? – Shelly Inc.

"But I was made by Ellyn Shic," protested Tumble. While Drone searched the Internet for intel on how Shelly Inc made T-shirts, Dot explained to him all about 'Smelly Shelly Belly' and her huge stores and their same-minute delivery drones.

"Maybe Ellyn Shic made you for her," wondered Dot. "How's it going, Drone? Taking a long time, isn't it?"

"Nothing... takes me... long..." strained Drone, pictures of T-shirts swirling on her screen. "This is just... trickyyyyyyyy..."

Eventually, she let out a mechanical sigh. "There isn't a single byte of **data** about Ellyn Shic," she muttered.

"But the Internet must say somewhere," said Dot.

"Actually, only 45 percent of people in the world have

Internet access, so it's not that surprising." Drone never missed a chance to correct someone. "This is the best I could find about Shelly Inc. T-shirt production."

She loaded the site onto her screen, but it was just a big yellow exclamation mark.

"Error!" blared Drone, reading the page out. *"You have searched for Shelly Belly and Ellyn Shic. Shelly Belly has nothing to do with Ellyn Shic."*

"Why would they say that if there really wasn't a connection?" wondered Dot, her detective senses on full alert. It was just like Sasser telling them not to waste their time. This was more than odd; this was suspicious.

"To the Detective Den!" Dot cried. When Tumble looked at her questioningly, she added, "Well all right, I mean back to my bedroom."

Chapter 6:

{The_Detective_Den}

"Drone, search CIAhub for case files on Ellyn Shic please," asked Dot. "And Shelly Inc."

"There's no data at all about Ellyn Shic, but look!" Drone flashed her screen with excitement. "Lots of open cases about Shelly Inc. Nothing definite though. One agent couldn't get into their warehouse. Another couldn't get into their offices. I wonder why she has such high security?"

"She must be hiding something," said Dot. "Drone, register our new mission on CIAhub. We're off to investigate Shelly Inc. They're clearly connected to Ellyn Shic, and she seems shady to me. We're going to find out how... and get Tumble fixed too."

Drone muttered that she was sure there'd be a reasonable explanation, that Shelly would be totally innocent and there were less dangerous ways to avoid getting into trouble with Dot's sister, but Dot wasn't listening. She was too busy laying out their strategy.

Plan:

Step 1: Snoop around the local Shelly Inc. store

Step 2: Discover how Shelly Inc. is linked to Ellyn Shic

Step 3: Find Ellyn Shic

Step 4: Learn how she makes T-shirts

Step 5: Get Tumble fixed

Step 6: Report back to CIA

"Couldn't be easier!" said Dot, ignoring Drone's worried mutters about the snooping. "Anushka will be back on Sunday, so there's no time to lose." Dot plotted the route to the nearest Shelly Inc. store using her selfie stick's **GPS**.

But before they could leave, they heard the front door. Dad was home. He barely allowed Anushka out alone and she was sixteen; he'd never let Dot go. Thankfully, she was prepared.

"HoloDoti, activate." Her ceiling light spun and twisted, and suddenly there appeared... Dot. Tumble gasped. "There's two of you!"

"Tumble, meet HoloDoti." Dot waved her hand through the second Dot. It was a hologram! The perfect double for when Dot sneaked out on adventures.

Dot set HoloDoti to homework mode, projecting the hologram onto her desk. Then she tossed a thick reel of cable out of the window, lassoing it around a fence post at the end of the garden.

"We can't just sneak out," fretted Drone. "It's against your dad's rules."

"I never agreed to them, so why should I have to follow them?" asked Dot.

"Rules are there to keep you saf—" Drone started, but Dot interrupted.

"If you don't like it, you don't have to come, Tumble and I will complete the mission on our own."

But Dot knew Drone would never want to be left out, so she scooped both her and Tumble up and ziplined down the cable with the selfie stick. No sooner had they hit the ground than Dot heard Dad up in her bedroom.

"How's the studying going, Odoti?" he asked.

"Hello, Father," came the voice of HoloDoti. "I am homeworking. I love homeworking."

"Good girl, I won't distract you!"

Dot heard him close her bedroom door. Easy peasy. She didn't think HoloDoti would be able to cope with a raging Anushka though – they'd better get going.

Chapter 7:

{Buy!_Who_Cares_Why?}

The Shelly Inc. store was massive. Very massive. Mega-massive. Ten double-decker buses tall, fifty lorries wide and covered in neon lights.

Gaping, they passed the Shelly Belly Fountain – a massive, ill-looking plastic micro-pig, squirting water from its mouth – and entered the mall. The place was even more gobsmacking inside. It looked like a whopping wedding cake, with five layers of supermarkets piled upon each other, covered in dollops of special-offer icing and sprinkled with flashing lights. There were gadgets everywhere, from Yo-yo-yoghurts (yoghurts on a string) to MagNets (fishing nets that attracted metal objects).

"Whoa," cried Tumble, awestruck by a hovering disco ball. "A million mirrors, all showing me!"

It had taken Tumble about ten distraught minutes to get his vanity back. "I'm still better looking than all the rest of you put together," he said.

Drone was more impressed by the Computer Window – glass you could surf the Internet on, meaning people didn't have to look outside at all.

"Watch it!" yelped Dot, as adult after adult barged past, arms full of new tech. Like Dot's Dad, everyone was carrying far too much – they kept bumping into each other, sending useless gadgets flying everywhere. Staff members rushed around too, piling ever more items onto shoppers.

"They're the staff?" cried Tumble. "They look more like models!" It was as if Shelly Inc. only hired people based on their looks...

"Yo, welcome to Shelly Inc. Stores!" screamed someone behind Dot. She spun round to see a uniformed teenage staff member with short hair and a grin. "Great deals guaranteed. Come and buy happiness!"

Dot thought this boy had bought a little too much happiness – he was practically shaking with glee.

"Hey, you're a girl, I bet you'll love this!"

he said, holding out a soft, squidgy doll. "Buy it. It'll make you happy."

"No thanks," said Dot. "Dolls aren't my thing."

"You don't like dolls? But..." The staff member's smile vanished for a moment. He pulled out a tablet and tapped something on it. Dot tried to peek, but the staff member held it away from her. "Heyyyy, you like computers, right!?"

"How did you know that?" asked Dot, surprised.

"Just a guess." The staff member quickly hid the tablet behind his back. "We've got a mega deal on all day: five laptops for the price of 14! How cool is that?"

"No thanks," said Dot again. "I'd love to look at your T-shirts though."

"T-shirts? Sure!" cried the boy. "This way!" Grabbing Dot's hand, he practically dragged her through the store.

The clothes floor was a maze of jumpers, dresses and jackets. Clothes flew off the rails as customers grabbed enough to fill a wardrobe twice over. The staff carried huge cardboard boxes of clothes, restocking shelves the second someone emptied them.

With fashion everywhere, Tumble was taking as many selfies as he was footsteps. Drone muttered that he was wasting memory.

The staff member finally released Dot's hand in the

middle of the T-shirt section. "How many T-shirts do you want to buy? Three for every day of the year? You totes don't want to be seen in the same thing twice, right!?"

"None, actually," said Dot, holding up Tumble. "I just want this one fixing."

"Don't be silly," giggled the staff member. "Buying a new one is way cheaper!"

Dot pulled a puzzled face. "But new ones need new materials, and I've got all the fabric here. If you make T-shirts, surely you can put them back together too?"

The staff member just shrugged his shoulders, his smile fading. Dot thought back to her CIA training – if an adult avoids your first question, keep digging. "Where do you make your T-shirts?" asked Dot.

"Try the website," said the boy, flustered.

"I have," replied Dot. "It had no info."

Quivering, the boy suggested calling the helpline.

"What's the number?" asked Dot.

"I don't know. Maybe you could send an email."

"Where to?"

The boy couldn't cope with so many questions. He let out a cry of "SECURITY!" and before Dot knew what was happening, a huge shadow fell over her, blocking out all the bright, flashing Shelly Inc. store lights.

Dot turned around. She wished she hadn't.

Looming over her was a security uniform. And in the security uniform was a tall, muscly, young woman, with cold, mean eyes. She cracked her neck and her knuckles.

Dot gulped. Drone beeped. Tumble quaked.

"She's asking questions!" cried the boy. "She must be another CIA spy!"

The security woman narrowed her eyes angrily.

Dot tried to say "I'm not a spy, I'm a detec—", but the security guard picked Dot up in one hand and plucked Drone out of the air with two fingers. Tumble rolled quietly into a corner, just a forgotten pile of fluff.

Chapter 8:

{Handy_Hanzi}

Thud. Dot hit the ground outside the shop.

Clank. Drone hit it, too.

Stomp. Stomp. Stomp. The guard marched back inside. Dot instantly leapt to her feet.

"We must be onto something here, Drone," Dot exclaimed. Drone slowly wobbled up to Dot's height, her rotors sputtering back to life. "Update the CIA on our mission – Shelly Inc are *definitely* hiding something."

"Roger that," replied Drone. "I'll log onto the CIAhub and…"

Suddenly, Drone's voice changed to a cold, steely tone.

"Warning – you are using Shelly Inc. **Wi-Fi** to access a banned website. You will be dealt with immediately."

Drone fizzed, buzzed and beeped, then every part of her turned off at once. Dot only just caught her before she hit the floor.

"Drone?!" cried Dot, cradling her in her arms and hammering her power button.

After what felt like a lifetime, Drone slowly lit back up.

"What happened?" cried Dot.

"I don't know," booped Drone groggily. "I think Shelly Inc. tried to shut me down with a **virus**."

"They really don't want us investigating them, do they?" said Dot. "All the more reason to!"

"You two left all of a sudden," chuckled Tumble, swinging the selfie stick as he skipped out. "Wanna see the photos I took?"

"No we do not," snapped Drone. "Our mission just became a lot more serious."

Tumble raised a stray strand where his eyebrow should have been.

"I'll take that as an excited 'YES!'," he said.

Dot and Drone weren't listening; they were too busy figuring out their next step. Dot wanted to march straight back in and demand answers, but Drone felt this was too dangerous – she wasn't risking another denting or a virus.

"Look at this awful stitching!" sneered Tumble, flicking through his snaps of the other clothes in the store.

"We could try to sneak into a staff-only area," suggested Dot.

Drone liked this idea even less. "We'll get worse than a denting if they catch us doing that!"

"The less said about this onesie the better," scoffed Tumble.

Drone rounded on him. "No one cares!" she shouted at maximum volume. "We don't want to see stupid photos of stupid clothes! We need a new lead."

"Hang on..." Dot's detective senses were prickling. "Tumble, did you get any close-ups with the clothes?"

"Yeah!" he cried, swiping through picture after picture of him pouting with different garments.

"Can I see?" asked Dot, holding out her hand for the camera.

Tumble was delighted. He grinned smugly at Drone as Dot zoomed in on picture after picture.

"It's no use, Tumble takes up too much of the frame," Dot sighed. "Wait, what's that?" In the background was a staff member with a big cardboard box.

Dot flicked through the pictures one after another. Tumble had taken so many, so quickly, that they could flick through and watch the staff member moving.

"It's like a flipbook!" said Dot.

"Or a GIF!" added Drone. "They're digital flipbooks."

The staff member went along the rails, hanging up

clothes from the box. Something was written on its side. "If only they'd come close enough for us to read what it says."

"There!" cried Dot. In the last photo the box was finally in focus. But the words weren't words. At least they weren't words Dot had seen before. "Run an image search online please, Drone."

"They're Chinese characters, also known as Hanzi!" explained Drone, seconds later. "I'll put them through a translator... *Voila!* It says - 'Made in Changsha, China.'"

"You've done it, Tumble!"

"I have?" said Tumble.

"He has?" said Drone.

"What have I done?" asked Tumble. "I know, obviously, but Rustbucket needs it explaining."

"You've found a lead! Shelly Inc. don't make T-shirts here. They make them in China!"

"Hey, what about me?" protested Drone. "I translated it."

But Dot's brain was too full of questions to listen to Drone.

"Why do that? Sending them over must take forever! And why hide it from us? There's only one way to find out," said Dot, pulling her 'I've-got-a-great-idea' face.

"Oh no," muttered Drone. Dot's great ideas were almost always dangerous.

"We've got to go to China!"

Chapter 9:

{What_a_Flight-mare}

"Wow!" cried Dot as they entered the hustle and bustle of the airport. Bodies dashed, screens flashed, speakers chattered, and suitcases scraped along the floor.

The last time Dot had been to an airport was when her dad had seen a deal for super-cheap flights and not read the small print. He, Dot and Anushka ended up on a one-way flight to the Sahara Desert. They were stuck there for a week, and their tickets home had cost four times the price.

Dot spotted people checking in with their e-tickets, scanning their phones under a laser. She didn't need one though – her CIA e-badge was a master-pass. She stuck it under the scanner and ping! They were through.

"It's that simple?" asked Tumble, astonished, as they waltzed through. "Why don't you jet off all the time?"

"I only do it for really important missions," explained Dot.

"And more importantly, Dot has school," snapped Drone.

Dot rolled her eyes. "Drone, log into the CIAhub. Hopefully there's an agent in China who can meet us when we land."

"Why can't we just assign the mission to them?"

"We need to get Tumble fixed, remember?" said Dot. "Plus, it'll be so exciting!"

Drone humphed to herself. Exciting definitely meant dangerous.

It wasn't long before they were on board the plane. Sadly, it wasn't exciting. It was just like a big bus, with seats on either side and an aisle down the middle. The screen on the seat in front for inflight entertainment was hardly advanced technology. Near the front, a curtain hid fancy First Class from sight – why couldn't the CIA e-badge get her a seat there instead?

An air steward stepped through the curtain and explained what to do in an emergency. He then asked everyone to switch their electronic devices to flight mode.

"Absolutely not," snapped Drone. "What if I get a notification? Or need to search something? No chance."

"Drone," teased Dot. "It's the rules."

"You can't break rules one minute then dangle them over me the next!"

"Hey, I'm following them," shrugged Dot, turning her phone off. "Are you, Tumble?"

"Of course! Look, I'm turning the camera off. No selfies for me, it's the *rules*," giggled Tumble, sitting on Dot's lap. He was enjoying Drone's dilemma. The pixels on her display, which formed the shape of a face, scrunched up, and she shot from side to side as she thought about what to do.

"Fine!" she cried, sucking in her antennae. She turned her propellor off, and fell with a thump into Dot's lap. Her display changed from pale blue to angry red.

The jet engines whirred into life and the radio piped up. A woman introduced herself as Captain Coleman and said that everyone needed to strap themselves in for take-off.

No sooner had Dot buckled up than the plane started rocketing down the runway. It was so speedy, Dot felt like she was stuck to the back of her seat.

But then there was an almighty *screeeeeech*. The plane stopped so suddenly that if Dot hadn't been strapped in, she'd have been the one doing the flying.

Dot looked out the window and was amazed to see a limo had pulled up alongside the plane. Out stepped two black sandals, black trousers, a neat white shirt, a gigantic grin and bleached white hair. It was...

"Shelly Belly," growled Dot.

"Where? Where?" cried Drone, springing into life. Shelly was skipping down the runway with a huge pile of money in one hand and her phone in the other so she could snap selfies. A steward approached her, and she dumped the cash on him.

"She's coming on board!" cried Dot.

All through the plane, the passengers gossiped and tittered. Were they really going to fly on the same plane as *the* Shelly Belly?

"This is why you need to clean me with a microfibre cloth!" moaned Drone. "She can't see me like this!"

Dot wasn't so star-struck. Why was Shelly Belly going to China?

Everyone strained in their seats, hoping to get a glimpse of the celebrity, but Shelly was ushered straight through the curtain into First Class.

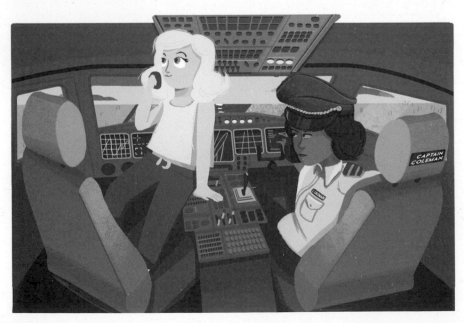

"Apologies for this delay, folks," crackled Captain Coleman over the radio. "We've had a very late arrival, and, er, she's bought the plane."

"Heyya guys, it's me, Shelly Belly! I'm so pleased to have so many lovely passengers. This trip will be totes more fun if you're all friends – so cosy up!"

The seat in front of Dot slid back, squashing her legs.

"Cosier!" Shelly screeched.

All the way down the plane, everyone's seats shifted back further, squashing them up so tight that their knees met their chins. First Class was now twice the size.

"COSIERRR!"

Even with her small legs, Dot felt like a shark in a sardine can.

"This doesn't seem like a very nice thing for Shelly to do," said Drone, confused by her heroine.

To make matters worse, the in-flight entertainment was awful. Shelly-sponsored movies! There were no jokes and no action, but the characters kept using Shelly's products over and over again. The movies lasted the whole fifteen stuffy, squashed hours it took to fly to China.

Chapter 10:

{Agent_An_Xing}

Changsha Airport's ceiling was so high, Dot wondered if they ever tried flying the planes indoors. It curved up and down, as if someone had frozen a sea wave, and there were huge glass windows everywhere.

"No time to waste," said Dot, rushing through the airport as quickly as her sore legs allowed. "We set off at 9pm, so it must be about 7am now."

"Actually," said Drone, "the time in China is seven hours ahead of Britain. It's mid-afternoon here."

"All the more reason to press on," said Dot.

As soon as they were out of the airport Dot stopped. They were here. China. Right in the middle of it.

China was huge. Vast. Eye-stretchingly enormous. Dot couldn't see it was 44 times bigger than the UK, but she could feel it. Even the light seemed different, as though someone had played with all the picture settings on a TV. It seemed softer, less crisp. It was grey, like England, but a different grey. A warmer grey, if grey could be warm.

The city of Changsha rose up ahead of them. Huge skyscrapers stood in rows along the horizon.

"That looks like a good place to start." Dot pointed towards the city. "Everyone keep your eyes peeled for our CIA contact. Drone, can you connect to a hotspot, in case they message us?"

After going ten hours without any signal, Drone didn't need telling twice.

"Connecting, connecting, connecting... ERROR!" Drone flashed red. "This connection is blocked. Odd, I'll try another."

Drone tried again – another error. And another, and another. For every Wi-Fi signal, every search engine and every website, they got the same big, red error. She was flashing like a Christmas tree.

"Aha!" Dot spotted a Chinese boy, not much older than her. He was sitting trembling on a bench on the side of the road, hiding behind a newspaper that was far too big for him. Dot approached the boy and whispered one of the CIA's coded greetings.

"What do you call a joey with a cold?"

"A kangAITCHOO," replied the boy nervously, peering over his newspaper. Dot smiled – only a CIA agent would know the answer. "How did you see through my disguise?"

"Your newspaper's upside down," Dot pointed out.

The boy blushed. "Whoops." He picked his phone up from his lap. "I haven't quite mastered hologram disguises yet." He pressed a button and the newspaper disappeared.

Giggling, Dot introduced herself. She didn't mention how well HoloDoti worked.

"I'm An Xing," he said. "Or you can use my English name, Marcus, if you prefer."

"Your English name?"

"We take on Western names for people not from China," explained An Xing. "Many people find them easier to say."

Dot wanted to know why he could speak English at all. "Don't most people here speak Mandarin?" she asked.

"*Wǒ men zuò de*. That's Mandarin for 'We do'. But I've been learning English at school since I was three," An Xing explained, as if it was the most ordinary thing in the world.

"I've only just started learning Spanish!" Dot was stunned. "I'm writing a translator plug-in for Drone, though."

An Xing spotted Drone. "Wow, nice bot!" He was even more impressed to hear that Dot had built Drone herself. "That's awesome! Does he have any games on him?"

"Him?!" cried Drone. "What makes you think I'm a *him*?"

"Drone's a *her*," explained Dot. People seemed to make that mistake a lot. "She doesn't have games, but she's got a super-fast processor, she's Wi-Fi connected, and she can fly, so she's pretty cool."

"I could surf the Internet too, if it wasn't all blocked," Drone grumbled.

An Xing apologised for offending Drone and explained why some Internet sites wouldn't let her on.

"Our government says they're protecting us from scary stuff, but cool things get blocked, too."

"That's like my school – we can't play games or watch

videos or message each other," said Dot.

They soon got down to their mission. Dot wanted to know the quickest way to the factory.

"I saw Shelly Inc. in the mission briefing," said An Xing. "I'm a bit confused. They don't have a factory here."

"But the boxes said they came from Changsha," said Dot. "Are there any other clothes factories in town?"

"Just one, but it's massive – have you heard of Ellyn Shic?"

Dot's eyes lit up. This was no coincidence – Shelly Belly and Ellyn Shic had to be connected somehow!

"It's this big, grey lump on the west of the city," continued An Xing. "I've heard stories about it. It doesn't sound nice."

"All the more reason to investigate," Dot said determinedly.

"If you're sure," shrugged An Xing. "I can take you there, but I won't sneak in with you because I, er, have to get home for dinner." (Not every CIA agent was as brave as Dot, but they made up for it with other skills.)

He chucked Dot a helmet.

"What's that for?" she asked.

"So you can ride on this!" he cried, pulling a moped out of the bushes.

Sticking the helmet on gratefully, she hopped onto the seat behind him.

"Strictly speaking, I'm not old enough to ride this," admitted An Xing. "But everyone here does, so sssh!" He winked. Dot grinned. Every CIA agent she'd met, even nervous ones like An Xing, had a rebellious streak.

Drone played an audio file of tutting. "But the rules are there to keep us sa—"

An Xing's moped roared into life, cutting off Drone, and they were rocketing down the road.

Chapter 11:
{Ellyn_Shic}

The road to Changsha was ten lanes wide! Dot had never seen a road anywhere near this size in Britain... and yet it was still clogged with a huge traffic jam. Thankfully An Xing and his moped were nimble enough to sneak through the tiniest gaps.

"I can't look," whimpered Drone, as they wove through the traffic. "I'm turning my video feed off."

"This is nothing," shouted An Xing, over the noise of a hundred engines going nowhere. "We've got one road that's 50 lanes wide and still gets traffic jams! Can you imagine?"

Changsha was unlike any city Dot had ever seen, even on TV. London and New York had lots of different tall buildings – some were pointy on top, some rounded, some 30 windows high, others a hundred. Here though, every skyscraper looked identical, as if someone had built one then copied and pasted it a hundred times. The houses were identical too.

"What a magnificent city," Tumble exclaimed. "They

must make their clothes somewhere very stylish indeed."

They soon left the traffic jam behind, entering the western part of Changsha. They rocketed down street after street until a huge grey block of concrete loomed up ahead.

"That's the factory!" An Xing cried, pointing.

Dot thought all factories would have smoking chimneys and pipes leading everywhere, but this one was just a big, perfectly smooth, rectangle. It was so grey, it looked as though it was trying to blend in with the sky around it and hide its size from everyone. There was one small row of windows about halfway up.

"Clearly, there's been a mistake," huffed Tumble. "I'm far too stylish to have been made somewhere as hideous as this. This can't be Ellyn Shic."

The moped turned the corner, and the next side of the factory came into view. Emblazoned across it, in letters the size of houses, were the words E L L Y N S H I C

Drone booped in amusement. "You were saying?"

Dot watched Tumble quiver slightly. It was as if a teeny little doubt had just dropped into his mind, like the face you might make when a tiny spot of rain falls.

"It must be a disguise," Tumble decided. "So people think that nothing stylish is made in there and don't steal their secrets." He didn't sound very confident though. Dot just wished she could figure out why Ellyn Shic seemed so familiar.

An Xing stopped right in front of the gates. They looked very big, and very locked. "Be careful in there, Dot," he warned, as she hopped off. "They've gone to great lengths to keep the CIA out, so I don't think they'll be happy if they find you've snuck in."

Dot thanked him for his help and gave him the special CIA secret handshake. Then, with a wave, An Xing went dodging through the traffic, back the way he'd come.

The gang turned their attention to getting inside. It didn't look like Ellyn Shic ran daily tours. There was no gift shop, and definitely no chance to get your photo on a keyring. A huge wall surrounded the factory, far too high and smooth for even Dot to think about climbing.

But there *was* a row of trees growing on the pavement.

"I wonder... " said Dot, clambering up the closest one. But it was no good. She was high enough to see over the wall, but too far away to jump. Besides, she'd spotted guards patrolling inside.

Dot was considering if there might be a back entrance, when there was a huge chugging noise. The gates clanked open and a big red lorry tore past the tree that Dot was in. It was like a huge metal skip, totally open on top, and Dot could see that it was full of wooden crates. It drove straight through the gates without even stopping. More guards kept watch on either side. The second the lorry was in, the gates crashed shut behind it.

"So the gates open for lorries..." An idea was hatching in Dot's brain..

"Oh no," said Drone, spotting Dot's great idea face again. "Don't even dare suggest–"

"We'll sneak inside the factory in a lorry!"

Chapter 12:

{Gate_Crashing}

Dot dropped down from the tree. The wall might be stopping her from getting in, but it also provided good cover from the guards – she was totally out of sight as she crept up to a metal control panel by the gates. It had a buzzer, an intercom, and a number pad for entering a passcode.

"All I need to do is reprogram the gates to stay closed longer," she said as she started unscrewing a panel. "There must be a way to define the time it takes to open and close them."

"Surely we want them to stay open longer?" Tumble asked.

Dot explained that they had no chance of getting past the guards on foot. "But if the gates are closed, the lorry will have to stop, and then I can probably jump into it from the tree."

"Probably?!" yelped Drone. "What if you miss? Or the lorry doesn't stop? This is far too dangerous, it might even cause an accident. The rules are there..."

"Stuff the rules!" said Dot, dropping the metal panel. "I thought you had artificial intelligence – why not use it to think for yourself for once?"

Dot was too busy fiddling with the circuitry to notice Drone's pixels glow a pained pink.

"If you're too scared then don't come," Dot continued. "Tumble and I will solve the case ourselves."

"Without her hacking and searching and translating?!" piped up Tumble. "I don't think so!" But Dot wasn't listening. She was too fed up with Drone being such a scaredy bot.

"I'm just trying to keep you safe," Drone whispered.

"I don't need keeping safe," snapped Dot. "I'm a detective, I can look after myself. Either stop getting on my nerves or get lost. I need to concentrate."

Drone's pixels scrunched in on themselves. She looked like she barely had the will to keep herself off the ground. She glanced at Dot once, then slowly hovered off, her underside almost scraping the pavement.

"Wait!" cried Tumble, but it was no good. Drone had gone.

"We don't need her," Dot huffed. "I can use my phone for everything. Watch how easily I reprogram this gate."

She fused her phone in. It sparked, giving her a little shock. Wrong connection. That never happened with Drone's universal adaptor. Dot tried again. *BUZZ*. Wrong again. *Buzz. Buzz. Buzz.* By the time she'd connected she'd been buzzed more times than a doorbell.

Dot wanted to change the code so that after the gates had detected a lorry, they wouldn't open for a whole minute. That meant changing the time **variable**.

Normally this would be pretty easy for Dot. But normally Dot had Drone. Now she only had her phone, and it was so slow!

"Aren't you done yet?" asked Tumble.

"It's the gate that's being slow, not me," Dot snapped. "And before you say anything, it's nothing to do with not having Drone."

"Reckon we'll be able to catch that lorry?" asked Tumble casually, pointing down the street at another huge Shelly Inc. truck that was chugging towards them.

"Oh no!" cried Dot, just as she finished the **code***. She grabbed Tumble and made it back up the tree at a speed a squirrel would have been proud of.

Climbing onto a branch, Dot crossed her fingers as the lorry approached, hoping the gate would stay closed long

*See page 120 for the Open_Sesame_Gate_Code

enough. But... what if the lorry didn't stop and crashed into the gate? Maybe Drone was right, maybe this was a bad idea...

There was a huge screech. Thankfully the driver had realised the gate wasn't opening just in time. The brakes had been thrown on with a squeal and the truck ground to a halt millimetres from the gate, straight ahead of Dot, almost two metres away. Just like the one Dot had seen earlier, the lorry had no roof and was filled with pile after pile of crates.

"It's a long way," said Dot. Longer than she'd thought.

"A very long way," agreed Tumble.

Dot was much better at high jump than long jump. Could she make it?

She looked at the road below, then wished she hadn't. They were higher up than she'd thought. If she missed, it would hurt. A lot.

"What are you waiting for?" demanded Tumble.

Dot took a deep breath. Her eyes were focused on the lorry, but her ears could hear the gate clanking. This was it. Any second now the gate would open and the lorry would drive off. This was their only chance. She had to go for it.

"Three... two... one..."

Dot jumped.

Chapter 13:

{We're_In!}

Everything had moved very quickly while Dot was preparing to jump. The second her feet left the tree everything went into slow motion. Dot felt like a fish swimming through glue. She was getting closer to the truck – but sinking lower and lower all the time.

'I'm not going to make it,' she thought. 'I'll miss it by a millimetre and go splat on the road.'

Then something grabbed her T-shirt from behind, lifting her just slightly so she could reach the rim of the open truck. With a huge effort, she dragged herself up, dropping with a thump onto a wooden crate. The next second the gates opened – if she'd left it any later, the guards would have seen her scrambling up.

"Whew, that took all my strength!" gasped Dot as the lorry drove up to the factory.

"And mine," whispered Drone, collapsing next to her. Her rotors weren't spinning and her screen was dim.

"Drone!" said Dot. "What are you doing here?"

"Saving our bums, that's what!" cried Tumble. "What a catch!"

"You know I'm too heavy for you to carry!" scolded Dot. "What were you thinking? That was so dangerous!"

"I thought you liked danger!" wheezed Drone. Catching Dot had drained most of her battery; she was now in power-saving mode. Her screen was dim and her volume was turned right down.

"Not when someone gets hurt!" said Dot. Then she realised – if it hadn't been for Drone, *she'd* have been hurt.

All the awful things she'd said to Drone came flooding back. Dot hadn't just been wrong, she'd been mean. She felt the bottom fall out of her heart, and hung her head in shame.

"About before... those things I said," she mumbled, not looking at Drone. "I didn't mean them."

"Think nothing of it," panted Drone.

"I'd be lost without you," said Dot.

"That's because you don't have **GPS**," whispered Drone. Dot smiled.

Metal clanked.

Metal clunked.

A gigantic garage door opened.

Dot shushed Tumble – they were here. She ducked down between the crates so that no part of her was visible. The truck pulled inside, then creaked and groaned one last time as it parked up.

They'd made it.

Chapter 14:

{Going_Loopy}

The second the truck halted, Dot was up and ready to go.

"Wait!" beeped Drone over the deafening grinding and scraping sounds of the factory. "We need to check that the coast is clear."

Dot was about to say that they didn't have time, but then she remembered how Drone was often right to be cautious. She sat back down in the lorry and waited. Seconds later, the driver climbed out, wearily trudging right past the spot where they'd have jumped down. Dot could see how tired she looked. It was a pity humans didn't have a power-saving mode.

While Dot waited, she inspected the crates. They all had a strange flag printed on them: thick blue, white and green stripes with thinner red ones, and a moon and stars.

"What country's flag is that?" asked Dot.

Drone scanned it with her camera. "Uzbekistan," she wheezed. "That's ten hours' drive away."

"What's come from there?" wondered Dot, prising open another crate. It was stuffed with ball after ball of soft, fluffy white material. Before Dot could ask what it was, Tumble buried himself in it, rolling around happily like a cat against its owner's legs.

"Cotton! I remember you now!" His memories were clicking together like plastic bricks. "Uzbekistan has field after field of cotton plants, and these balls grow on them, like little clouds! Children and teachers would pick them all day long."

"Wait, so you travelled all the way from Uzbekistan to China to be made into a T-shirt, then got sent to Britain? That must have cost a fortune! But Shelly Inc. shirts are dirt cheap – how's that possible?" Dot wondered.

Drone had her own suspicions. "I thought you said you were silk?" she asked.

Tumble stopped rolling in the cotton. Dot saw him shiver, as though another raindrop of doubt was running down his back. She wondered how he was coping with these surprises – first the factory hadn't been what he'd expected, and now this.

"Who cares what I'm made from," he shrugged, shaking the doubt away. "It's how amazing I look that matters."

Dot decided the coast must be clear by now, and scooped Tumble up before he and Drone could start bickering again. She hopped out of the lorry, and Drone hovered slowly after her.

Dot scurried through the factory, crouching so low that her head was almost the same height as her knees. Tumble clung to her back and Drone flew low behind them. Getting caught by someone now, when they were so close, would be awful. The factory was spotlessly clean and the lights were so bright that there wasn't a single shadow to hide in.

"Watch out!" cried Drone. A CCTV camera stuck out from the ceiling, slowly rotating, scanning the whole corridor. Dot ducked round a corner before it could spot her.

"This place probably has cameras everywhere," whispered Dot. "We need to shut them down before one spots us."

A cable was trailing from the camera. Dot traced its route along the ceiling, round the corner and down the corridor until it disappeared behind a locked door. A quick twist of the selfie stick's digital lockpick and the door swung back to reveal a huge control panel. There were dozens of screens showing what every camera could see. The entire factory was laid out before Dot.

"Psst!" said Dot. "I was wondering if you could help me?"

The control panel opened one bleary eye. Dot explained their important mission to investigate Shelly Inc. and fix Tumble, and how crucial it was they remained unseen. Could the control panel pause the screens? Just for an hour or so?

"Are you out of your mind?!" roared the control panel. "I can't go breaking rules for every kid who comes wandering along."

"I'm a CIA agent," said Dot, flashing her e-badge.

The controls scoffed. "Kids can't be CIA agents."

Dot had to deal with this problem a lot. She tried explaining that this was a very different CIA, but the control panel didn't care.

"If you won't break the rules, I will," muttered Dot to herself. "Drone, I've got a little favour to ask..."

Drone rolled her pixels. "At least this time breaking the rules might keep us safe..." she reasoned, lowering a cable from her body. Dot grinned, activating the screwdriver hidden in her selfie stick. She unscrewed a big metal plate from the controls, revealing its circuit boards. The machine sparked as Dot fused Drone's cable to the circuitry.

"Oi! Stop that!" barked the controls. "I'll sound my alarm."

"Oh yeah?" said Dot, waving an unplugged speaker.

"If you dare rewrite even one line," started the machine, but Dot was already tapping away. "I mean, please rewrite my programs. That is a good idea."

Dot giggled. The control panel sounded like HoloDoti now. A little **coding*** later and Dot was done.

"I don't get it," Tumble was inspecting the screens. "They all look exactly the same."

"Exactly," said Dot. "If I turned all the cameras off, someone would notice. Instead, I've put a **looping** code in. The cameras will play the same 30 seconds of footage over and over again."

"Wonderful, incredible, almost as great as me!" cried Tumble, watching a guard patrol the same patch of grass again and again. "It's magic!"

"Nope, just coding," grinned Dot.

*See page 122 for the CCTV_Don't_Get_Me code

Chapter 15:

{Keeping_up_with_Fashion}

Dot didn't know what route to take, but she didn't have much choice – nearly every door was locked, so they passed through the ones that were open and hoped they were going the right way.

As they crept along, they passed bedroom after bedroom, each with 12 bunk beds squashed inside. Did the workers have to sleep here as well as work?

A noise grew louder and louder as they tiptoed down the corridor. A buzzing sound, with some thumping thrown in for good measure.

"We must be getting close!" whispered Dot. "We'll find out how you were made in no time, Tumble."

They turned a corner and suddenly found themselves in a gigantic hall. The ceiling was high enough to fit a tree in quite comfortably and everything was gleaming white. Dot thought it looked a bit like a hospital. There were long lines of people, all working on huge tables. The closest person to them was a girl who couldn't have been much older than Anushka. Hunched over a sewing machine,

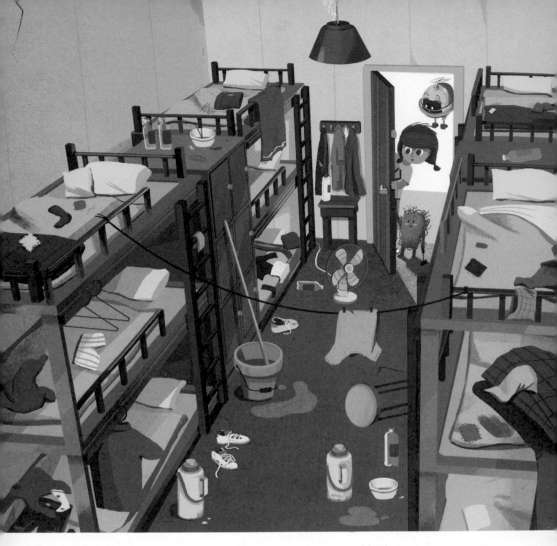

her hands whizzed to and fro. She was working frantically, barely stopping for breath. The gang moved forwards to get a better look. The girl was sewing T-shirts! So were the people next to her.

The gang scooted down the line, where women and men were making T-shirt after T-shirt. They all wore white overalls and little white caps, almost like people in fish and chip shops. They were so focused on their sewing that no one gave Dot, Drone and Tumble a moment's attention.

"This can't be right," muttered Tumble, the raindrops of doubt turning into drizzle. "I couldn't be mass-produced like this!"

"Look out!" cried Dot, grabbing Drone and Tumble, and diving under a table.

No sooner had Dot tucked her feet under than – *ziiiiiip*! – something shot past in a blur, thundering to a stop in the middle of the hall.

It was a hoverboard.

The hoverboard gleamed and sparkled in the bright lights – it looked as though it was made from solid gold. Above it were two shiny black sandals, one pair of pitch-black trousers and 100,000 bleached-white hairs. All that added up to one Shelly Belly. Her micro-pig was following her on its own mini-hoverboard, like a dog behind a butcher.

"But the website said Shelly Inc. had nothing to do with Ellyn Shic!" cried Drone, her screen turning a furious red. "She's lied to us!"

"Listen up, guys," trilled Shelly to the workers.

The workers continued churning out T-shirts.

"Whoopsie, you haven't learnt English," giggled Shelly.

"Eh? An Xing did!" whispered Dot.

"Maybe they went to a different school?" wondered Tumble.

"Maybe they didn't go at all," suggested Drone.

Shelly pulled a MagNet from her pocket and a megaphone flew towards her.

"Yo, stop right away please!" Shelly blabbed through the megaphone. It wasn't any old megaphone, though. It was a ShellyBelly Translator-later Megaphone. It waited until she finished talking, then repeated everything in Mandarin. Some workers stopped, but others seemed too desperate to finish the T-shirts.

"Naughty naughty, don't forget Cool Rule One: stop when I say!" tinkled Shelly. "Pretend it's a break!"

Everyone stopped dead still. Shelly started slowly driving up and the down the rows of tables.

"You guys remember Awesome Logo Design 307, yeah? The one you've been stitching into tees for the last five fun-filled days? Sucky news – I've decided it's out of fashion. Soz. Cool Rule

Two: we're never out of fash! Let's change it right away with no delay, yay!"

The workers grumbled and groaned to each other.

"Cool Rule Three, guys: no complaining! You love your jobs, remember?" Shelly wagged her finger. "But do say if you've got a suggestion!"

No one dared raised their hand. No one dared step out of line. Dot scowled. She did not like the way Shelly was treating everyone.

"If you guys wanna be paid for all these T-shirts then you'd better unpick the old logos ASAP and sew the new ones in!"

The staff were lost for words. They would be basically making each T-shirt twice, yet only getting paid once. And it would take so long! It was so quiet you could hear a pin drop.

"Cool Rule Five: No pin dropping!" sang Shelly sweetly. She tapped away at her tablet computer. "You'll find the wicked new logo on the Shelly Inc Hub with the others. Ready? Set? Sew!!"

"Hear that?" whispered Dot excitedly. Every staff member pressed a button on their sewing machine. A little built-in tablet lit up and downloaded the new design. "We can find Tumble's design on their system!"

That was easier said than done, though. Shelly was

circling the factory floor on her hoverboard like a great white shark. There was no way they could reach the server without Shelly spotting them.

"We need something to grab their attention,"

whispered Dot.

Tumble swept back his threads and twirled his selfie stick.

"If there's one thing I know about," he said, "it's attention."

Before Dot could ask what he had planned, he was gone in a flash – a camera flash. Seconds later, a flash went off across the factory floor. Then one went off on the opposite side. Flash after flash, Tumble dashed around the factory, photographing anything and everything (but mostly himself).

"Spies again!" cried Shelly. "So not cool!"

In an instant, Shelly's hoverboard was shooting after the flash.

This was Dot's chance. She and Drone scurried up to the server, plugged in and synced up. Before they could access any files, she needed to guess Shelly's password. It wasn't *'Imastupidface'*. Nor was it *'Badbreath7'*. What could it be?

"She loves selfies, so maybe she's so obsessed with herself that her password is..."

"Shelly," typed Dot. No luck.

"I don't think a trillionaire inventor would be silly enough to have her own name as her password," said Drone.

"Wait!" Dot had an idea. She typed Shelly. Then she typed '1'...

Ping! They were in.

"People really need more secure passwords," tutted Drone. The letters 'Ellyn Shic' spun around on her screen and Dot finally realised what she'd been missing.

"Look!" she tapped on her phone. "Rearrange the letters Shelly Inc. and you get Ellyn Shic!"

Drone was too busy searching through the data, byte by byte, to be annoyed anymore at Shelly Belly's tricks. 0s and 1s swarmed her screen.

Dot kept watch, but Shelly was still too busy chasing

Tumble's flash. Images started forming on Drone's screen.

"Trousers, shoes, hoodies..." Drone was filtering through the data. Every now and then a human face flashed among the clothes.

"That's weird," said Dot. "Why's she been designing faces?"

More and more faces flashed up, until they started outnumbering clothes. Dot racked her brain for an explanation. "Wait, what's that?"

Drone opened the file on her screen. Staring out at Dot was her dad. There was all sorts of information about him in graphs and charts. They knew his name, his age, his height, even what he watched on TV, what he searched online, and what he'd bought from Shelly Inc.

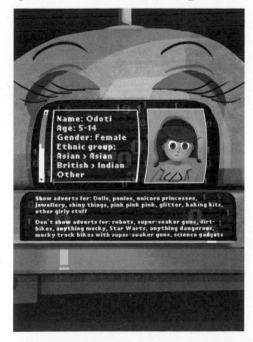

"How do they have all this?!" Dot was stunned.

"It gets worse." Drone flicked on to the next face – it was Dot's! More graphs, more information.

"They've been spying on me!" Dot was outraged. Spying was meant to be her job.

"Spying on everyone!" added Drone. "There are millions of these files!"

Dot gave the info a closer look, and realised it wasn't all correct.

"Their entire database is like that," said Drone. "They think every girl likes dolls and every boy likes video games. That'll be why the sales assistant was so sure you'd like a doll."

Before Dot could start ranting about Shelly Belly, a little voice chirped up behind them.

"Phew, I'm zonked. All this running calls for an exercise selfie! #witnessthefitness!" panted Tumble, sweating heavily. "Shelly must have given up by now, right?"

"Tumble!" protested Dot as he pouted and posed. "You'll lead her over here!"

Too late.

"I'd love to know what you're doing in my factory," trilled a sickly-sweet voice behind Dot.

Chapter_16:

{Shelly_Belly_Showdown}

With a gulp, Dot turned around. There was Shelly, all smiles.

Drone was still searching through the files. Dot needed to stall for time. She plucked up her courage and said:

"I'm investigating."

"How fun! Find anything cool?" Shelly asked.

"I've discovered all about your secret factory," Dot told her. "You can't hide behind computer viruses and fake names any longer. I'm going to tell everyone all about it!"

Shelly flared her nostrils up so much that Dot could see her nose hairs. Dot braced herself – surely Shelly would fly into a fit of rage. But she didn't. Instead, she giggled. A chilling, horrible, giggle.

"You think you're a spy. Isn't that cute?" giggled Shelly. "If you weren't just a silly little kid someone might believe you."

"I'm not a silly little kid. I'm Detective Dot, CIA!"

Detective Dot flashed her official CIA Detective e-Badge. Shelly clapped her hands in glee.

"I've been dying to meet the CIA. You're much more trouble than stupid old grown-ups," sniggered Shelly. "I hate to disappoint you, dear Dotty, but no one cares how I make my inventions or where they come from. They buy from me because I'm impossibly cheap."

With a sinking feeling, Dot realised that was true. But it wasn't the only one of Shelly's secrets she knew.

"Oh yeah? Well I don't think they'll be happy when they find out that you've been spying on them," Dot retorted.

Still no fit of rage. This time Shelly just raised an eyebrow.

"Don't act like you don't know!" Dot snapped. "I've seen your database; you've got info on everyone!"

"Bless!" chuckled Shelly. "That's not spying. People's Wi-Fi devices give me that data. Everyone's agreed to it, it's on page 22,113 of our Terms and Conditions document."

'What?" exclaimed Dot. "People never read that!"

"That's the point – duhhh!"
Shelly was getting smugger by the
second.

"Found it!" pinged Drone as
she downloaded a design to her
hard drive. Shelly's eyes snapped
towards her. "Whoops..."

"Been stealing my data, have
you?" asked Shelly. "Now that *is*
naughty."

page 22.113 of 161.515

Condition 2.355: In accepting these terms
and conditions you promise unconditionally
and for all time to allow Shelly Belly and
her friends and family and pets and pets'
of pets to stay at your house for free
without notice and on demand
("the accommodation"). And to give her
all of your data ("your data").

If you breach any of these terms, Shelly
Belly reserves the right to be anything
from mildly angry to completely furious,
in which case Shelly Belly will at all times
be entitled to the sole use of any one of
your arms and/or your legs for any such
purposes as Shelly Belly thinks is fair.

©Shelly Inc.
All Rights Reserved

Shelly whipped out her MagNet. She squeezed the
trigger, and Drone was instantly pulled into the coils of
wire. Shelly laughed as she reeled her In.

"You can't hurt Drone!" cried Dot.

"But she'll have such lovely info on the CIA! And
afterwards she'll make wonderful spare parts," said
Shelly, grinning like a Cheshire shark. "I'll turn her into a
sewing machine and sew your mouth shut."

Drone beeped frantically, but the magnets were too
strong. She couldn't move. Shelly advanced on Dot
menacingly. She was much older than Dot. Much taller.
Much bigger. Dot couldn't hide her Level 11 Scared Face.
What could she do now? Even if she could escape, she
couldn't leave Drone. The staff had all stopped working,
watching what was happening with worried eyes.

Dot felt something jabbing her back. She glanced down

to see Tumble poking her with the selfie stick.

Dot gave Tumble the tiniest of grins, taking the stick from his outstretched threads. Her Level 11 Scared Face transformed into a Level 10 Great Idea Face.

"You're not going to wipe my selfie stick too, are you?" she asked innocently.

"Been snapping my factory? Tut tut," squealed Shelly. Another squeeze of the MagNet's trigger, and the selfie stick shot out of Dot's hand.

"Oh no! Give it back!" shouted Dot, trying to hide her grin as Shelly twirled the selfie stick in her hands.

"Selfies are my super fave! I can capture my victory against the CIA!" Shelly gloated.

Shelly's thumb hovered over the thumbprint sensor. She was too busy grinning for the camera to see Dot and Tumble clamp their hands over their noses...

Shelly pressed the button.

When Tumble had triggered the MegaFart back home it had been brewing for roughly 30 minutes. Shelly's had been brewing for over a day. The one from Dot's room smelled like roses by comparison.

The MegaFart knocked Shelly clean out. She collapsed with a gasp into a crumpled little black and white heap on the floor.

Dot leapt up, hand still pinching her nose shut. She

powered down the MagNet. Drone shot up out of it, and the gang raced off.

Weaving around astonished workers, Dot ran back through all the twists and turns they'd taken on the way in, skidding around corners and dashing through doors. It wouldn't be long before Shelly was awake – they had no time to lose.

Dot ran into the garage where she'd first entered. The doors were sliding open and a truck was revving its engine, about to leave. Dot leapt up a huge pile of boxes and crates as though jumping up a giant's staircase. She didn't need Drone's help this time. She was high enough, close enough, and moving fast enough – she dived into the lorry and landed with a thud on a crate.

Escape!

Seconds later, the truck drove off. They'd made it. Just the small task of getting from China back to Britain, and then she could expose Shelly Inc. Oh, and fix Tumble.

Back in the factory, Shelly groggily came to. Rubbing her head, she clambered to her feet.

"I hope no one's slacking off," she trilled. "Get back to work!"

Chapter_17:

{Mission_Complete}

The gang were in luck. Their escape truck had a delivery for Shelly Inc. UK. They hid in the crates and spent the flight in the aeroplane's hold.

After what felt like forever, the plane finally touched down in England. Dot ran home as fast as she could. With no sunlight, Drone had run out of power on the flight before they could find Tumble's design. Would they have time to find it and fix him before Anushka came back?

Dot climbed up the cable and in through her bedroom window. HoloDoti was still at her desk, ploughing through homework.

"I still can't believe how awful Shelly Belly really is," said Drone, transferring the Shelly Inc. design data to Dot's computer while she recharged. "And to think, I used to like her!"

Dot smiled. They might have different views on danger and rules, but at least she and Drone now agreed on Shelly Belly.

Dot uploaded the design Drone had downloaded,

praying it would have something, anything, that might help her fix Tumble before her sister came back.

"I won't be in a mass-produced design," sighed Tumble. "I told you, I'm unique!"

No sooner had he finished bragging than a picture of a bright blue T-shirt appeared on Dot's computer. Huge letters called it a 'Standard, basic smar-T-shirt'.

"But, but, but... I'm one of a kind!" Tumble whined, scrolling through the file desperately. "I'm the latest fashion!"

He found the product info. *'Produced April. Discontinued May. Reason: Out of fashion.'*

Dot winced as Tumble read the words over and over again. Everything he'd believed about himself was a lie. He looked as if he'd been dreaming of  a wonderful feast but had woken up to find only cold broccoli for breakfast.

"There might be instructions on how to make you, though," said Dot, trying to cheer him up.

"What's the point?" moaned Tumble. "Even if I was fixed I'd still be unfashionable."

"You're still Anushka's favourite T-shirt. She doesn't

care whether you're fashionable or not. We have to fix you before she's back."

The front door crashed open. "I'm home!" shouted Anushka. "Have you missed me?!"

That was it, then. They'd failed to fix Tumble. Now Dot had no choice but to tell Anushka the truth. She dragged herself downstairs.

"Did you enjoy your study weekend?" she asked, miserably.

"What on earth are you talking about?" asked Anushka, forgetting all about her cover story. "Oh, wait, study weekend... yes! It was... super fun..."

"We've had a great time," said Dot's dad, none the wiser. "Odoti's really behaved herself, none of her usual mischief or anything!"

Dot shrugged. "Nush must be a bad influence on me."

Anushka laughed, and crouched down to give Dot a hug.

"Someday I'll show you how to sneak out of the window," she whispered to Dot.

"Now you're back, Anushka, I can rush off," said Dad. "Shelly Inc. have a sale on Tablet Tablets. Tiny touchscreens you swallow!" He was gone before Dot could say how stupid that was.

"So, what have you actually been up to?" asked Anushka. Dot didn't know what to say, so she said everything at once, very quickly.

"Nush I'm really sorry but I was cleaning Drone and your T-shirt got caught and I dunno how but it fell apart and I tried fixing it but that made it worse so I'm really sorry I'll buy you a new one when I've saved enough pocket money except they don't make that one now so it would have to be a different one."

After a long pause, Anushka said "Which T-shirt?" It looked like she was trying to decide how angry to be.

"Your blue one," said Dot, avoiding eye contact. To her amazement, Anushka just laughed.

"What, that cheapo Shelly Inc. one? Eww, I never wear it anymore – it's got a computer chip in it – that's not vintage. I'd forgotten I even had it, don't stress about that!"

"Well do you mind if I keep the cotton?" Dot held out the tangled ball.

"Sure." Anushka rolled her eyes. "Whatever."

Back in Dot's room, Tumble twiddled his strands sadly.

"Too old to be trendy,

not old enough to be vintage," he said. "I'm not unique, not special, not even wanted."

"Don't be like that," said Dot, giving him a hug. "You're super special. You're funny and daring and the best photographer I've ever met. And you found a major lead!"

"I'd never have the guts to distract Shelly like you did," added Drone.

"You didn't just distract her. Your quick thinking with the selfie stick stopped her! You saved me! So did you, Drone," said Dot. Both her friends beamed with delight. "And you are unique, Tumble. Just think, that factory churned out millions of T-shirts, but there are no other balls of cotton walking around, are there?"

"You're right!" Tumble exclaimed, jumping up, full of beans and bounce. "I am fantastic! I am superb! And wonderful and dashing and ever so pretty."

"That's not quite what we said..." corrected Dot. "As for unwanted, we want you. Don't we, Drone?" Drone was clearly trying to think of a smart answer. "Don't we, Drone?" Dot repeated.

"Oh yes, really want you. Absolutely," the little robot said drily.

"I'm not finished with Shelly Belly. Everyone needs to know about her. We have to investigate a lot more. You can be our official crime scene photographer!" said Dot.

Tumble leapt up so high in excitement that he grabbed the light shade.

"You'll have to build me another selfie stick!" he said, swinging from the ceiling. "With HD video. And sound recording. I could have my own MeTunnel channel: Detective Tumble and his less attractive friends."

"If anyone wants me, I'll be in standby mode," Drone groaned, turning her screen off with a huff.

While Tumble continued dreaming of glitz and glamour ("Has there ever been a T-shirt superhero before?") Dot sat down at her computer to type up her CIA Mission Report. It was vital that the CIA found out about Shelly's operations as soon as possible.

Dot normally did as little as possible for her homework, but CIA Mission Reports were different – she actually liked doing them. She put in every detail she could think of, from the personal data that Shelly Inc. had collected, to Shelly buying the plane and the conditions in the factory. She also researched the Uzbekistan cotton fields Tumble had mentioned in case the CIA wanted to send someone to investigate them, too.

The CIA had agents all round the world, and they were recruiting new ones all the time. If a child asked a lot of questions that adults wouldn't answer, and were brave, they were probably perfect agent material.

"There," said Dot, attaching a picture of Shelly the

second the MegaFart hit her nostrils. She logged into the CIAhub and pressed upload.

Bwark! Error. But the CIAhub never had errors... A pop-up appeared with a picture of a horrible, tiny pig.

"We can't have you uploading that file now, can we?" giggled the pop-up.

A familiar logo exploded onto the screen. Shelly Belly had hacked the CIAhub! Dot gasped in horror as file after file was deleted from the system, right in front of her eyes!

That settled it. Shelly wasn't going to get away with this. Dot hadn't been to China and back just to fall at the final hurdle. She, Drone and Tumble knew more about Shelly and her tricks than anyone else in the CIA – and maybe the world. It was up to them to stop her, even if it meant staying up late. *Especially* if meant staying up late.

First step? Boot Shelly out of the CIAhub.

"Wake up, Drone," said Dot, already typing as fast as she could. "We've got some coding to do."

WARNING!

The following content is not appropriate for adults.

_Children's Intelligence Agency

Think for yourself | Question everything

The CIA is a secret, hi-tech intelligence agency run by kids. Adults don't always tell us the truth, and almost always underestimate us. Our agents investigate global mysteries, criminals and rotten teachers around the world. We will stop at nothing in pursuit of the truth!

Areway ouyay ookinglay orfay ethay uthtray ootay?

Ancay ouyay eepkay away ecretsay?

Ancay ouyay eadray isthay?

Ontactcay usway!

_The CIA Code of Conduct

We kept it short:

1. Question everything

2. Think for yourself

As a CIA operative, it's your solemn duty to fight unfairness, protect people and the planet, and investigate where farts come from and how they're made.

Who makes rules? Do we have to follow them? What is privacy? Is it okay to spy? Is everyone equal? Should kids go to school? Is everything you read, see, and hear true? Why do some people lie? How do you know what is true? How do you know who to believe?

_Top Secret: Agent Profiles

_Detective Dot's File

Personal Details

Name: Detective Dot

Codename:

Rank: Detective

D.O.B: 23 March

INTERNAL ONLY MEMO

Description/traits

Particulars:
Female, 133 cm tall, 29 kg, brown eyes, brown hair. Scar on left knee

Skills:
Coding (languages include: Ruby, LOLCODE), inventing, playing video games and eating crisps at the same time, ziplining

Weaknesses:
Doesn't like following ANY rules (sometimes a strength), takes uncalculated risks, never finishes homework on time

Disposition:
Curious, tenacious, determined, brave, rash, reckless, rebellious, thinks outside the box

Special abilities:
Can talk to technology

Mission record:
Unavailable due to security reasons

Security clearance
LEVEL 5

_Top Secret: Agent Profiles

Personal Details

Name: Miss Drone

Codename: <ol>/<a>

Rank: Sidekick

D.O.B: 24 August

Description/traits

Particulars:
Carbon fibre and titanium
shell, 45 cm high, 1.6 kg,
single pro-copter, 1080p
screen

Skills:
Searching, flying, spying,
accessing the Internet,
data retention

Weaknesses:
Scares easily, relies
heavily on Wi-Fi,
quick temper

Disposition:
Loyal, hardworking,
obeys rules, strict.
NOTE: Obsessed with Drone
Racing League – a real
petrol head.

Special abilities:

Mission record:
Unavailable due to
security reasons

Security clearance
LEVEL 5

_CIA-approved Spy Equipment

_Dot's Selfie Stick

INCLUDES: LED torch, GPS locator, Wi-Fi access, fingerprint sensor, USB logger (insert it into a computer and it will record everything anyone types into it!), hard drive, tinkering equipment (screwdriver, spudger etc), toxin sensor, touch-screen, universal translator, conversation monitor, voice recogniser.

<u>Do not pick nose before using</u>

If you insert the USB logger into a washing machine, it will break. Don't insert it into a washing machine.

★ **Constant monitoring mode**
_the selfie stick will film / listen / radar everything all the time.

★ **Artificial Intelligence mode**
_the selfie stick is able to make predictions based on millions of data points.

PATENTED

_Tech Tats (Beta)

Electrical components can monitor the heart rate, blood pressure and body temperature of the wearer

Invisible, wireless, digital tattoos

Use skin electrodes to read people's facial expressions (by monitoring muscle movements)

Self-powered using sweat

PATENTED

Can scan entry into locked rooms with digital keys

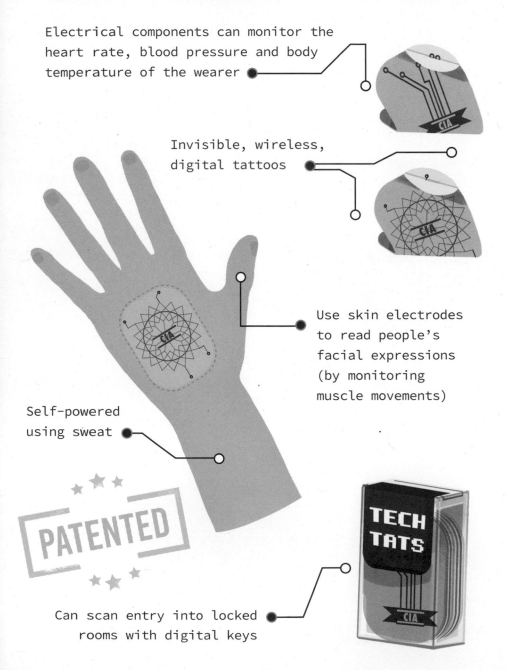

_The Holodoti v1.2

This hologram is used by Detective Dot for at-home cover. It has four different modes - sleeping, homework, tidying and monitoring (so Dot can use it as an extra pair of eyes at home). Dot can control it remotely when she's out on missions.

Got an idea for an awesome gadget? Get in touch!

EXCERPTS FROM AGENT D. DOT

REPORT: Operation 5636, Changsha

*** CLASSIFIED ***

Urgent Update: Following the completion of Operation 5636, I attempted to upload my report and discovered the CIAhub had been hacked by Shelly Inc. Thanks to the quick response of agents at HQ, we were able to block the attack. We are now working to increase our online security. And get rid of that stupid pig from the front page.

I recommend all agents change passwords. This cyber attack was a deliberate act of aggression from Shelly Inc., and we need to investigate immediately.

_Spying On Us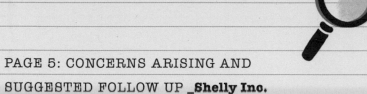

PAGE 5: CONCERNS ARISING AND
SUGGESTED FOLLOW UP **_Shelly Inc.**

Shelly Inc. is spying on people everywhere!!! She's tracking
the websites we visit, videos we watch and games we play.
She's acting all nicey-nicey by having free Wi-Fi in her shops,
but if you log on, Shelly Inc. takes data from your phone.
Drone says it's technically legal, but they're still being very
sneaky about it. NOT COOL.

Shelly must be spying so she can sell more stuff. I tested
our theory by visiting fakevom.com – soon every video I
watched was swamped with adverts for plastic sick. Worse
still, Shelly Inc. thought that because I like sick I must be a
boy, so I started getting adverts for stuff like water pistols
'for boys'. How can a water pistol be just for boys? What's
the difference? It's so stupid, I don't like particular toys just
because I'm a girl. I'm old enough (and smart enough!) to
think for myself, but what if I was younger?

They don't stop at spying, they're brainwashing too! The
characters on Frenemies (the BEST TV show!) eat Shelly
Jelly all the time and it makes me really crave it. I bet
Shelly Inc. pay them to eat it just to make me want it. It's
mind control!

_Factory Fails

The Ellyn Shic factory seriously sucked. Everyone works crazy long hours without breaks, and Drone went on and on about all the fire hazards and dangerous chemicals, AND there aren't enough laws to protect people. It's nothing like home.

We interviewed Wang Weo*, who looked about the same age as Anushka (17). Wang Weo grew up in a small village, leaving school when she was 13. She moved 700 miles (a two-day drive!) to Changsha, getting a job at Ellyn Shic because she needed money to feed and house her family back home. She lives in a tiny factory bedroom, squashed in with other workers, and she only gets paid 2p per T-shirt. I couldn't believe that! Worst of all, she had to leave her baby, Mei Ling, behind, because it was too expensive to take her. Mei Ling lives with her grandparents and only gets to see her mum on national holidays.

Wang Weo told us that she's never been on the Internet!!! Can you imagine that?! Drone did some research and we discovered that only half the people in China have Internet access, even though it has the largest population on the planet. Also, the Chinese government decides what websites people are allowed to see – YouTube, Google and Facebook are all blocked! That seemed really strange – we use Google so much that 'to Google' is in the Oxford Dictionary.

*We changed her name because she'd get in loads of trouble if her bosses found out she'd told us about the factory.

_Uzbekistan

When he'd recovered his memory, Tumble filled us in on
Shelly Inc.'s cotton. It's grown in Uzbekistan for 200 days
before it's picked. The crops are sprayed with pesticides to
keep insects and disease away, but that makes the workers
ill. Tumble used to see children in the cotton fields too.
Drone said they should be at school (but maybe it's fun not
to have to go to school?) It takes the cotton ten hours in a
lorry to reach Changsha.

_Smooth Sailing

We couldn't believe how far T-shirts like Tumble travel to reach shops in the UK. Tumble likes calling himself a globetrotter but it's terrible for the environment! The boat that took him from China to the UK was powered by oil, which releases carbon dioxide and causes global warming. Tumble seemed unaware of global warming when questioned, which we found surprising. He's really not very observant, except when it comes to selfies. Global warming is killing plants and animals, and it's terrible for everyone. EVERYONE says global warming is terrible... we're taught about it at school. So how come our clothes are made so far away? It doesn't make sense.

_Action

_ Why don't people care where Shelly Inc.'s T-shirts come from? It's weird because everyone I know would be really upset to see how awful the factories are, and they wouldn't want a T-shirt made like that, even if it was really cheap. So, what's going on?!

_ I spoke to Aunty Harjeet and she says she can't afford more expensive clothes. She also said that nothing will ever change, but that it was 'sweet' of me to care. That's the problem with adults, they can be SO STUPID. Obviously nothing is going to change if nobody changes anything. Duh. But things will change if we change things. It's simple logic. Double duh!

_ Every 'big' problem is just made of lots of little ones. Like an algorithm. So, logically, if we all change little things, then big things change. This means we need to investigate what little things we should do.

	China	Uzbekistan	UK
Distance from UK	7,788 km / 4,839 miles 74,171 football pitches**	5,050 km / 3,138 miles 48,095 football pitches**	0 km / 0 miles Not even a dribble!
Cost of loaf of bread	£1.22	£0.34	£0.94
Cost of 1 kg of rice	£0.76	£0.94	£1.28
Age kids leave school	14	16***	18
Population	1.357 billion	30.24 million	64.1 million
Minimum wage per hour	Average: £1.54 Depends on location, season and amount of garments made.	£0.47	25+: £7.20 21–24: £6.70 18–20: £5.30 Under 18: £3.87
Hours worked every day	11 hours per day, 6 days a week. This can increase to 18 hours during peak season.	12 hours per day up to 6 days per week during peak seasons.	6.4 hours per day with weekends off.

* Figures collected in 2016

** Measured from goal to goal

*** But kids miss weeks of education each year when their teachers have to work in the fields. Kids pick cotton sometimes too. Even though Uzbekistan made child labour illegal in 2014, our on-the-ground agents have evidence to show that kids are still being forced to work.

_Code with the CIA

The CIAhub is a secret database of all the Children's Intelligence Agency's inventions. It shows agents how to turn everyday objects into super spy gear. It also lets us work together on new inventions, **debug** and improve existing gadgets, and re-use useful algorithms.

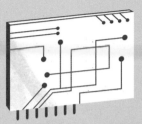

The API (AY-PEE-EYE) is the thing that gives agents access to a whole load of clever functions so they can build stuff. It's like a website, sort of.

Think about a robot. A robot can do lots of different things and can have a lot of different functions. A robot might be able to have a conversation with a human, hoover a room without bumping into walls, pick its nose, or complete a homework task.

However, in order to do this, a human needs to write the instructions for the robot so that the robot knows exactly what to do, because a robot can't think for itself – it's pretty dumb! It's a computer, and it only understands how to follow instructions in its own computer language, which is called code. If we want a computer to do something, we have to translate all our instructions into code.

Once we've written the code, other agents can use identical code to get their robots to do the same thing, or similar things.

NOTE: In school, teachers often say that copying work is cheating. But the CIA think re-using code is the same as recycling, and it's a big part of teamwork. What's the point of doing something twice? Agents are happy to share and use each other's code, which is called 'open source'. Maybe homework should be open source too!

Please see the source code to our CIA inventions below, for agents to use as they see fit.

Happy white-hat hacking!

_Detective Dot's Code

`Selfie_Stick_Code`

This is the code Dot created for her fart-making selfie stick. It's how the selfie stick knows if it should let someone use the cool spy gadgets, or if it should trigger the MegaFart instead. It's called an authentication code.

Plain text code

Before a computer can understand the code, the human writing it needs to understand what she or he wants the computer to do. So first, we write out the code in plain text. It means nothing to a computer, but a lot to a human!

Defined Terms

`cia_agents =`

this is a private list of CIA agents. Dot and Drone are on the list, obvs. These are the people allowed to use the gadgets.

`baddies =`

this is a private list of CIA suspects. These are the people who trigger the MegaFart or other defence mechanisms. Shelly Belly is high up on the list!

`lookUpUser =`

read through the two lists

Then, we write down the instructions for the selfie stick. This helps to organise our thoughts.

Plain Text Code

1. Read the thumbprint

2. Check the user's thumbprint against the two lists (baddies + cia_agents)

3. If the thumbprint belongs to a cia agent then unlock cool spy stuff

4. If the thumbprint belongs to a baddie then release the Mega Fart

5. If the thumbprint doesn't belong to a cia agent or a baddie then behave like a normal selfie stick

Algorithm

Next, we turn each instruction into the language the computer can understand, i.e. code. The lines of code create a set of instructions for the computer to follow, in exactly the order it's written in. This set of instructions is called an algorithm.

The computer reads the algorithm and does what it's told.

- When you see a hashtag, it means whatever text follows is meant for a real-life human to read, BUT the computer should ignore it. It's not part of the algorithm and therefore it's not an instruction. Coders use the # to make a note for themselves or their friends. Like a sticky note!

```
01
02
03    #This function is run when
04    someone touches the selfie stick
05    def checkUser(thumbprint):
06
07        cia_agents = ['dot', 'drone']
08        baddies = ['shelly_belly']
09        name = lookUpUser(thumbprint)
10
11        if name in cia_agents:
12            unlock(cool_spy_stuff)
13        else if name in baddies:
14            release(mega_fart)
15        else:
16            return
17
18
19
```

def - this tells the computer that the code underneath it is a new function, and it gives the new function a name. So you don't have to keep writing the same lines of code again and again, you can just use the name of the new function. For example, if you made a new spy-TV-remote and you wanted it to release a MegaFart if it ended up in enemy hands, you could reuse the checkUser(thumbprint) function when writing the code.

else: return - this basically means do nothing. Go back to normal. Here, normal is just being a normal selfie stick.

() - these brackets are for inputs. All functions might have an input, and if they don't, you leave the brackets empty.

Here, the input is someone's fingerprint. It could also be their voice, or a password, or anything else!

This is the code Dot created to make sure the gates at the factory in Changsha stayed closed for a bit longer, so she had time to jump onto a truck and sneak in.

Plain Text Code

1. If someone enters the correct entry code for the gate (1234)

2. Then stay closed, or 'sleep', for 15 seconds (to give us time to sneak into the lorry!)

3. After that, open the gate

4. Stay open for 60 seconds before closing again

5. But if someone enters the wrong entry code, don't do anything

Algorithm

```
01
02   #the number of seconds the gate should stay closed
03   before opening
04   close_duration = 15
05   open_duration = 60
06
07   def gateDoor(entry_code):
08       if entry_code is '1234':
09           sleep(close_duration)
10           openGate()
11           sleep(open_duration)
12           closeGate()
13       else:
14           return
15
16
```

The amount of time the gates will close and open are
variables. If we wanted, we could make people wait
5 minutes before the gates opened, by changing the
number to 300 in the close_duration variable:

close_duration = 300

But that would be really annoying for anyone trying
to enter! They'd have to wait 5 minutes!

CCTV_Don't_Get_Me_Code

This is the code Dot created so that she wasn't caught by the CCTV cameras when the gang were sneaking about in Shelly Inc.'s factory in Changsha.

Plain Text Code

1. Record a 30 second CCTV video without Dot, Drone, or Tumble in it

2. Keep playing this video in a loop through the screen, so that anyone watching the screen can't see Dot, Drone, and Tumble sneaking around

3. Stop playing the video at midnight, as the gang will have left the factory by then. Go back to playing live CCTV instead

Algorithm

```
01  #This function is to make sure the gang are not
02  captured on CCTV
03
04  MIDNIGHT = time(hours=24)
05  old_video = camera.scan(seconds=30)
06  #Take a 30 second video without Dot, Drone or
07  Tumble in the camera
08
09  #Now, loop and play the old video until
10  midnight passes
11  while time.now() < MIDNIGHT:
12      camera.play(old_video)
13
14
15
16
```

'While' means keep doing something for as long as a
certain thing (i.e. condition) is happening. Here,
the condition is that the time is before midnight.
So, as soon as the time is past midnight, the code
won't run. Until then, at the end of every loop, the
computer will check the time again.

Loops can either go on forever (While True), or for a
specific number of times, or until a certain thing has
happened (For or Until).

MIDNIGHT is in capital letters because it will never
change. Midnight is always 12 am.

_Training Modules

Tea-making Algorithm

Tea breaks are an essential part of undercover work. That's when a lot of thinking happens.

<u>Recap!</u>

You'll remember, computers can only understand code. So when we want them to do something, we need to talk to them in code. Each code is an instruction, and lots of lines of codes is an algorithm – a set of instructions. A computer does stuff in the order you tell it to – it does each line of code, then the next, and so on. Like a recipe.

First, to help us plan our code, we figure out what the instructions are in human language. So here are the steps you'd take to create the perfect cup of tea.

1. Collect together teapot, tea-bags and mugs;

2. Plug in kettle;

3. Place tea-bags in teapot;

4. Boil kettle;

5. Add boiling water to teapot;

6. Wait until the tea is brewed;

7. Pour tea into mugs;

```
8.  Add milk/sugar; *
9.  Serve.
```

* This depends on what sort of person you are. We've heard some people add milk before water. Weird.

Choices: milk or sugar

But what about the fact that some people want milk and sugar, and others don't? Often, we want computers to be able to make a choice and do different things depending on that choice. So let's say the choice is whether to add sugar:

```
1.  if(sugar_wanted):
2.        # then add sugar
3.  else
4.        # don't add sugar
```

More generally, the code for choices looks like this:

```
1.  if(condition):
2.        # then statements
3.  else
4.        # else statements
```

Loops: add water until kettle is full

When we add the boiling water to the teapot, we only want to do that until it's full. Not forever, or there would be a huge mess! We can do this by introducing a 'loop' – an instruction to repeat something WHILE something else is happening, or FOR a particular amount of time, or number of repetitions.

```
1.  while (kettle is not full):
2.          # add water to the kettle
```

More generally, the code for loops looks like this:

```
1.  while (condition):
2.          # do something
```

Loops: add tea to each mug

We might want the loop to only last for a particular amount of time (clock time), or for a certain number of times (repetitions). Here, we want the program to pour the tea into each mug separately.

```
1.  for mug in set_of_mugs:

2.         # pour tea into each mug
```

More generally, the code for loops looks like this:

```
1.  for a thing / time / repetition (e.g. a mug
    in a set of mugs / 30 mins / 10 times):

2.         # do something to the thing
```

So now we have a better tea-making algorithm:

```
1.   plug_in_kettle()

2.   teabag_in_teapot()

3.   while kettle is not full:

4.          add_water(kettle)

5.   boil_kettle()

6.   pour_kettle()

7.   sleep(60)  # Wait for 60 seconds
     while the tea brews

8.   pour_kettle()

9.   if sugar_wanted:

10.         add_sugar()

11.  else

12.         pass  # pass means "do nothing"
```

```
13.
14.  for mug in set_of_mugs():
15.        pour_tea(mug)
16.  serve()
```

Training task 1:

Create an algorithm for: going to bed at night, packing your bag for school, making a peanut-butter sandwich... or for something extra-complicated, create an algorithm that will let you know when an adult is coming near your bedroom! This will help you hide any secret plans just in time.

Include at least one conditional statement and at least one loop. If you send this to the Children's Intelligence Agency HQ, we will consider your application to join the CIA favourably. If you've already created your own algorithms, we'd love to see them too.

ALGORITHMS

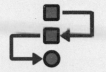

An algorithm is a list of specific instructions to follow in order to solve a problem. The order of the instructions is important. Think about an algorithm for getting dressed in the morning. What if you put on your trousers before your pants? That would be silly! Imagine showing a robot how to brush its teeth so it can learn how to do it itself (imagine if robots had teeth!). You would need to explain every step, in the right order, so it will understand and not get confused.

The instructions would go like this:

1. Open the toothpaste
2. Put a bit of toothpaste on the toothbrush
3. Open your mouth
4. Brush your teeth for 2 minutes
5. Rinse your mouth with water
6. Smile and say 'AAAHHHHHH'

So that's the algorithm for brushing your teeth. But for a robot to understand the instructions, you'd need to translate them into computer-language – code!

CODE

Computers don't understand words; they understand code. Words come in different languages – English, French, Russian, Gibberish – and code does too, such as Python, Ruby and Scratch.

Computers only do what we tell them to do and only understand instructions in code. The instructions need to be very precise or the computer will make a mistake – it can't think (unless it's been told exactly how to)!

A whole set of instructions is called an algorithm.

COMPUTER

A computer isn't just a thing with a screen, keyboard and mouse – an oven, a digital watch or a robot is a computer too. Anything that takes in instructions and follows them to create a result is a computer. This is called input-process-output. Computers:

1. Input data
2. Process it (i.e. follow instructions)
3. Output information.
4. If you set an alarm clock to 3 am and leave it under someone's pillow, that's the input. The alarm clock waiting until 3 am is the process, and the alarm sounding and waking someone up is the output.

Think of your oven:
- Input: setting the time, temperature, on/off switch
- Process: oven heats up, switches off at a particular time
- Output: hot oven = yummy food.

Think of your smartphone:
- Input: touch screens, cameras, GPS, or microphone could be the input
- Process: e.g. if you take a photo, save it to the Camera Roll
- Output: screen, speaker, headphones, vibrations

DATA

Data is raw information. It's a group of facts or statistics (facts in number form) that we can use to understand something. For example, you could collect data about the types of TV programmes your friends like to watch. You could use their answers to find what the most popular programmes are.

DATABASE

A collection of information on a computer that is stored in such a way that you can use it and add to it easily. It's really important that you can search the data quickly and efficiently, otherwise your database is rubbish.

DEBUGGING

Finding and solving mistakes in computer programs is a bit like ironing the creases out of clothes. Why is it called debugging? Rumour has it that in 1947, scientist Grace Hopper's computer wasn't working properly. She found a moth inside it, and when she took the bug out it fixed the system!

GPS

A navigation system involving satellites and computers that can determine the location of people on earth. It stands for Global Positioning System.

HACKING

Digital trespassing! Finding your way into a computer system that you don't have permission to be in. It's pretty naughty, like sneaking through a ticket barrier. Some people hack to do bad stuff, such as stealing data that doesn't belong to them. White-hat-hackers use it as a force for good.

INPUTS

What you put into a computer, whether it's a button press, a mouse click or a whole program. It's like putting cake mix into an oven – the input gets turned into other things.

INTERNET ACCESS

55 per cent of people in the world don't have Internet access. Without it, you can't contact people freely, you can't share knowledge and you can't learn from others. Imagine your life without the Internet!

LOGICAL REASONING

A way of working things out, by saying that one fact must be true if another fact is true. Or sometimes, you can say that if one fact is true, another fact is probably true. When Dot was trying to guess Anushka's password, she thought that as the letters printed on some keys were worn down, it was probably true that Nush touched these more than the other ones, and as she had to type her password in all the time, it could be because of that.

LOOPING

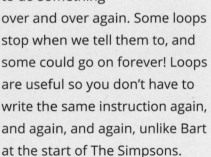

Loops are a code that tell computers to do something over and over again. Some loops stop when we tell them to, and some could go on forever! Loops are useful so you don't have to write the same instruction again, and again, and again, unlike Bart at the start of The Simpsons.

PATTERNS

A pattern is the same order being repeated over and over again. When you lay the table, you know one plate goes with one knife and one fork. Once you know that, you can repeat it without spending time thinking. It's the same with computers – spotting patterns saves a lot of time.

PERSEVERING

This is where you keep going and never give up – like reading right to the very end of a book about a young coder, her robot sidekick and a talking T-shirt.

In tech, persevering is really important, because 98 per cent of time is spent testing and debugging. And in life, persevering is one of the most important things to do.

PROBLEM SOLVING

This is a special skill that requires logical thinking and perseverance, among other things. Problem-solving skills are used all the time in our daily lives. How do you get somewhere if your bus is cancelled? How do you build a fort using only the items in your bedroom? What should you do if you left your homework at home and your teacher is going to kill you?

SYNTAX

There are some words that are recognised by all computers,

whichever coding language they use. This is the computer's syntax.

The words below mean something specific to a computer.

You'll see :
- def – create a definition
- do/call – carry out a task
- input – indicates that here the user will be inputting something
- print (output) – indicates that an output will appear on the screen
- return – this is the completed task. It tells the computer to end that bit of code.

You can also use math operators such as:
- +, –, <, >, AND, OR, . . .

And there are loops/conditional statements:
- while – a loop code that keeps repeating itself WHILE some other condition is being met
- for – a counting loop

- if/then/else – a decision (selection) in which a choice is made
- repeat until – a loop (iteration) that has a condition at the end

TESTING

Testing is checking everything works – like rehearsing a school play to check everyone knows their lines. It's a big part of coding. For example, with the CIA selfie stick, If Dot's dad buys a new TV, the selfie stick might not recognise it any more, so she has to test it.

VARIABLES

A variable is data that could change. The exact number of crisps in a packet, your high score on a game, or how much money you have in your piggy bank are all variables. When Dot hacks the gates so she can sneak into Ellyn Shic, she changes the time variable so it stays shut for longer.

VIRUS

A computer virus is a bad set of instructions that make computers do things they're not meant to do, such as shut down, or delete important files.

WHITE-HAT HACKING

Hacking is not allowed, but white-hat hackers believe they're doing it for a good cause. It's like Robin Hood stealing from the rich to give to the poor. The CIA and Dot see themselves as white-hat hackers. Dot knows she shouldn't mess with Anushka's laptop, but she decides the mission is important enough to make it OK in the long run.

Companies sometimes encourage employees to white hack into their own systems, to make sure they are as secure as possible, and will give money as a reward for breaking in (a bug bounty). In 2016, Facebook paid out a £10,000 bug bounty to a 10-year-old kid called Jani! We cannot confirm or deny whether Jani is part of the CIA.

Some people think white-hat hacking is good (Dot!); others think it's wrong (Drone!). You have to decide for yourself.

WI-FI

A way to access the Internet over the air! 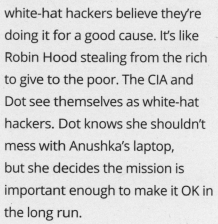 There's no need to plug in to anything, because a network is created in a particular space (the Wi-Fi zone) which lets you access the Internet (or more precisely, data) using radio waves. Wi-Fi zones can stretch to around 100 metres.

"I survived three weeks alone in the jungle thanks to this book."
Alara, aged 9¾

"My whole class read this book. I was stunned when they told me, in the strictest confidence, that ███████ ████████████ █████████!"
Sharna, teacher KS1

"At last, a book with this title."
Stephen, parent

"Before I read this book, I hadn't read this book!"
Cookie, book reader

A note from Sophie

Grown-ups have always told me that my ideas are 'sweet', but naive. They've told me I can't really change *things*. I'm just one little person, and, for example, choosing not to buy bottled water is hardly going to change the world. But that doesn't make sense. Of course nothing changes, if no one changes! If we make changes, everything changes. In a way, it's really that simple.

So what do I want to change? For starters, in cartoons, 0% of princesses are coders, boys are twice as likely to take the lead, 73% of characters have white Caucasian skin (compared to only 15% of people in the world!), and 92% of female characters are underweight. Plus, not one superhero recycles. That's not right.

There's other crazy stuff going on too. Why is a tub of posh ice cream made in England more expensive than a new T-shirt made in China? It doesn't make sense. We're becoming switched off from the reality of what's actually going on around us. But, deep down, most of us would like things to be different.

Stories shape how we think about ourselves and the

world. From the moment we pop out of the womb, we're bombarded with subtle and not-so-subtle messages about our gender, race, sexuality and visibility. Currently, those stories show us that if you're white and male, you're more visible. They tell us that if you're a girl you should be an air stewardess, not a pilot, and if you're a boy you can't like pink. That's not right either.

That's why I joined the Children's Intelligence Agency. Adults can be boring, and say stupid things about how nothing ever changes; they don't always tell the truth, and sometimes they don't even notice what's going on... and they certainly don't ask nearly enough questions. So I'm proud to be an OAA (Older Aged Agent) for the CIA. If anyone can get to the bottom of this nonsense and really make a change to this world, it's kids.

Sophie Deen

Lawyer, techie and school counsellor, Sophie Deen is the founder of Edtech company Bright Little Labs and the creator of Detective Dot. She was voted Computer Weekly's 'Rising Star' and the British Interactive Media Association's 2016 'Innovator' for her work in bringing gender equality to kids' media. Before setting up Bright Little Labs, Sophie worked at Code Club, alongside Google and the Department for Education, to help introduce the new coding curriculum. Sophie is passionate about holistic, creative education for children, the empowerment of underrepresented groups, technology, and sustainability.

Very big, very heartfelt thanks

We could not have done this without the support of our families, friends, amazing Kickstarter backers and all the extraordinary, wonderful people who've been so generous with their time, advice, and loveliness along the way.

You are the original D-Team and we love you.

****

A. Blackburn, Ada Oliveras Puigarnau, AB, ABW, Adrian & Theodore Klang, Adryana Daniels, Agata Lewicka, Ajay Patel, Ajay Sanghani, Alex Kayyal, Alexa Davidson, Alexander Koelbl, Alfie Stone, Alice Emmeline Helen Seymour Gamson, Alice Helena Mitchell, Alice Seymour Gamson, Alistair, Allison Salmon, Alysa Selene, Amahra Spence, Amelia & Eleanor, Amelia Lockwood, Amir H. Hajizamani, Amit, Amy DuFault, Amy Harbin, Amy Jussel, Amy Lewis-Adams, Andres Amaya, Andrew Carr, Andrew Morgan, Andrew Shields, Andrew Telson, Andrew Wolfin, Andy Lulham, Angie Maguire, Anish Chhibber, Anna C, Anna Leisz, Anna Ryon, Anoushka Deen, Arianna, Atrela, Aurora & Leonardo, Ava Garside, Ava Koso-Thomas, Becca Richman, Bella E. Danon, Bella W, Ben Sandhu, Bibi Elhadef, Bjørn Ola Smievoll, Bridget Kaya Brickert, Bori Kiss, Brother, C. R. Leonard, Caitlin & Alix Correll, Calumn Gunn, Camille Nelson, Captain Cybear, Carmen Maria Marin, Carola Garrecht, Caroline Hardman, Carol Pinkus, CC, Chakshu Saharan, Charles Putman, Charlie Trainor, Charlotte Finn, Charmian Love, Chris Dowdeswell, Christina Bolognini, Christopher Vollick, Claire Stone, Clara Emma Kelly, Clare MacDonald, Cloie Gorski, Coraline Salmon, Cosima Salim, Cristian Parrino, Damien Scully, Damilola Odusote, Daniel Benton, Danielle Katzir, Dan Thwaites, David Gaston, David Irwin, Dee Saigal, Derek 'D' Proops, Dexter Godfrey, Diana and Amara: House Corvidae, Dina S Willner, Dionne Bird, Diya and Isha, Doki Technologies, Dora Jack Fidler, Dr Abanus, Duncan Sommerville, Eleanor Lang, Elia & Alix Suppe, Elise Norman, Eliza M., Elizabeth, Elizabeth & Annabel Whelan, Elizabeth lazarus, Elizabeth Joy Barrass Chapman, Ella Benton, Ellie Hale, Ellie Scout, Elliott Lansdown-Bridge, Emily & Nathan, Emma & Mia, Emma Townsley, Emma Von Cooper, Emma Murphy, Emma Newcombe, Emmie Faust, Ena Straw, Enni & Aapo Laine, Esme and Caitlin, Ethan Hyman, Ettie Purdye, Eugene Greenwood, Evelyn Mae, Everyone at BGV, Ezra Jack brown, Florence Ayres, Fong, Francesca Harris, Gabriella & Abraham, Genie Ruzicka, George Flather, Georgie Frost, Georgina Wren Harms, in memory of Gloria Freedman, Graham Brown-Martin, Greg Annandale, Hannah Lyssa Smith, Harper & Eoin Barrett-Trounson, Harriet Napier, Harriet Shields, Harrison & Lydia Suchy, Hayle Davis, Helen Greenwood, Honor Mishcon, Hurricane Hurley, Isaac 'Will It Work' Dansicker, Isaac Riviere, Isabella & Georgina Hurley, Isabelle Deshon, Isla Fitz, Ivy Rose Sambol-Rickler, Jack Benton, Jack Stone, James, James Dellow, James Isilay, James Tweedie, Jamie Mason, Jana Völkel-Kitzmann, Jane Guest, Janine Guenard, Jasmine Johnson, Jeanne Phelan, Jenny Dorward, Jessi Baker, Jess Wade, Jessie Jacobs, Jo Baker, Joe F, Johan Adda, John Blair, John

Whiteworth, Johnanna, Jojo Tickles, Jolie Liner, Jonic Linly, Jordina, Joy Dardin, Joyce Deen (aka Dot's Grandma!), Judith Telson, Julia Barbour, Julia Lilian Miller, Julian Susana Naomi, Julio Terra, Julius RK Sowu, Kallen, Kari Wood, Kate and Bizzie, Kate Hammer, Kate Hyman, Kate Robinson, Katerina Georgiou, Katherine Gardiner, Katherine Warner and Victoria Hagins, Katheryn Wise, Kat Vambe, Kaylee Rogers, Kayleigh Bateman, Kela Rackind, Kenan McGrath, Kendal Fish, Kennedy and Jackson Guenard, Kennedy Pettygrove, Kerry Eyre, Kiera Gregory, Kieran and Liam, Kiernan Sjursen-Lien, Konnie Taylor, Kris Haamer, Larissa, Laura Kirsop, Laurence Leyens, Lauren Hyams, Lauren Kaufmann, Lauren Samples Bartholomew, Laurent Marchal, Lee Correll, Lee Delplanque, Lee Rickler, Leo Campbell, Lexi, Lexi & Leah, Leys Family, Liane Dabbous, Lily & Harry, Lily-Annabella Olufunwa, Lisa Bobroff, Logan Forsberg, Louise Bloom, Luca Malik, Lucia, Luciana Berger, Lucy Gill, Lucy McKillop, Luke Samble, Luke XJ Emmel, Lyla Jacobs, Macarena Mata, Madison Scully, Maë and Grisch, Maia Szczudlik-Bernard, Mark Berlin, Mark Featherston, Mary Moncrieff, Matt Desmier, Matteo Menapace, Matthew Guest, Matylda, Max Keenan, Max Koelbl, Maya Ghosh, Maya Malachi, Meliora, Melissa Denton, Melissa Karaviotou, Menahem, Mia Hadrill and Jessica Kettle, Michael Mentessi, Mike Jerome, Mike Royston, Miki Chojnaka, Miles Berry, Mina Margrethe, Mitul Thobhani, Molly & Moira Featherston, Monster Connolly, Moo, Morrison Benckert, Mysha Takeh, Naomi, Natasha, Natasha Allen, Natasha Frills Saxberg, Neel & Ravi Gupta, Neill Vandenberg, Nell Andrews-Hodgson, Nerea Martinez Sanchez, Nicholas Adrian Smith, Nicholas Bolt, Nihaal Basit, Nick Kind, Nick Telson, Noah Campbell, Noah Diner, Nora Bennett, Nora Lambert, Ole Sandbæk Jørgensen, Oryah Hametz, Paria Kamyab, Patricia at The Design Trust, Paul Andrew Hallett, Paul Elmer, Paul Hallet, Paul Kirby, Pavlina Draganova, Pete Penguin, Pete Trainor, Peter Young, Philip Kenley, Phil Neighbz De Semlyen, Phil Watkins, Phoebe Smith, Phoenix Cole Dyer, Polly Kenley, Poppy Pearce-Smith, Princess Millie Neumann, Priscilla Laurence, Rachael Benton, Rachel Davis, Rachel Vecht, Raf Goovaerts, Rebecca and Lucy Collinson, Rebeka, Reianna Peets, Rick & Fi Jones, Ricky Blair, Riley Maier, Rina, Rivka, Leah, Sarah & Moshe, Robie Unlacke, Ro Olufunwa, Rob Le Boutillier, Rocky and Phoenix Starr, Romica Prasad, Rory Graham, Mitchell, Rosalie Lorch, Rose Edmands, Ross Freedman, Rukesh Patel, Russ Shaw, Russell Allan, Ruthi, Ryan Petrich, Sadie Benton, Safia Minney, Sakari Deichsel, Sakina, Sam Couillaud, Sam Five, Sam Voulters, Samantha Best, Samantha Crase, Sarah Chapman, Sarah Corbett, Sarah Davies, Sarah Drinkwater, Sarah Sandbæk Vestergaard, Scarlett, Scarlett Chaney, Seema and Kirin, Sharna Jackson, Shervin Shaeri, Sibelle Zenkner, Sifar Jirgale, Sin Nii Leong, SmartSchool, Sofi Merino, Sonia Ben Ali, Sophia, Sophia and Parker, Sophia Bruni, Sophia Robertson, Sophie & Charlotte Utech, Sophie Berry, Sophie Kirkham, Sophie Sharpe, Sophie Snider, Sorcha & Tias, Space Princess Maggie, @spirals, St Monica's Primary School, Stefan Zenkner, Stephen Bennett, Stephen Deen (aka Dot's Grandpa!), Stephen Goodman, Steve Williams, Sue Black, Sue Deen, Susan Johnson, Suzy Breaden, Suzy Crook, Suzy Q, Sym Roe, T. Pirk, Tamara Kuzminski, Tasha Harbin, Tathem Lennox, Teague Size, Team Smesh, Temel Oktem, Teresa Gonczy, Tessy Britton, The Atlas Family, The Elaskys, Theo & Abs, The Korer Kids, the lovely team at Bethnal Green Ventures, the MacDs of New Brunswick, Theresa Rose, Tiana Parmar Bruno, Timothy Winchester, Tom Judd, Tom Quick, Turgay Oktem, Uncle Rob and Auntie Carole, Ugg, Vicky Hart, Uncle Mark, Vikki Fry, Vivek Narayan, Warren Cooper, Wendy E Rowe, Wilkie & Fredi Larke, Will Bentinck, William & Benjamin Croupe, William & Matthew Chaney, Yacine Baroudi, Yasmin Ali, Ylin Roy, Yusra Budraa, Belinda Parmar, Zachary Weeks, Zane Henry, Zaneta Stepien, Zikmanis Family, Zoe Alexander

Peace, love, and code.

For   Polly   Kenley

you   are   a   ☆

with lots of ♡♡♡

Sophie been